RAMPAGING FUCKERS
OF EVERYTHING ON THE
CRAZY SHITTING PLANET
OF THE VOMIT ATMOSPHERE

MYKLE HANSEN

Eraserhead Press
Portland, OR

ERASERHEAD PRESS
205 NE BRYANT
PORTLAND, OR 97211

WWW.ERASERHEADPRESS.COM

ISBN: 1-933929-78-2

ACKNOWLEDGMENTS

The title "Rampaging Fuckers of Everything on the Crazy Shitting Planet of the Vomit Atmosphere" comes from the song of almost the same name by THINKING FELLERS UNION LOCAL 282—the weird and fantastic San Francisco bizarro-rock band whose albums were played constantly during the writing process. Long may they shred!

I owe tremendous thanks to my dear friends Ralph and Patty Jazskowski, for the last-minute loan of their mountain writing studio during the completion of "Journey to the Center," and likewise to my dear friends James Bohem and Hanna Nelson for their use of their coastal bear observatory. Drinks for all my friends!

CONTENTS

MONSTER COCKS

For Carl and Rose

Tue Aug 05 20:37:52 PDT 2008:

Life is short, cruel, and uncertain, but this I know: I have got to get a larger, longer, thicker and more satisfying penis—AS SOON AS POSSIBLE!

I have MALE SEXUAL PROBLEMS. No sex whatsoever, for instance, is an enduring PROBLEM of mine. But I understand now that my enduring virginity is just a symptom, and the PROBLEM lies elsewhere. I get it now, what it's all about, but the knowledge came slowly. It took a lifetime of lying to myself about the secret importance of so-called chivalry and sensitivity and being "special" and "different." And waiting, alone. And jerking off, which is actually kind of difficult for me—not at all like it is for Rod Girder, star of the original MONSTER COCKS and narrator slash producer of MONSTER COCKS TWO through NINE, all of which I own, all of which I have watched, alone in my hiding places, all of which are available for immediate download from www.monstercocks.com. All of which describe an existence the exact opposite of mine.

We live in a futuristic wonder-world where a larger, longer, thicker, more satisfying penis is available for immediate download. So why should I stew in my SEXUAL PROBLEMS? The Old Me used to try to jerk off while watching Rod Girder swing around his monster cock on laptop DVD, play the piano with it, lasso vaginas with it ... the Old Me imagined I was "Lightning" Rod Girder, while imagining Rod Girder's co-stars Andrea Assbury and Lana Liason as duplicate copies of Angela Fine from Payroll—who is six feet tall and has skin like milkshakes and huge, delicious-looking breasts and who wears a side-slit skirt and heels around the second floor and is so totally sexy and totally nice at the same time—and the Old Me would imagine her moaning, in a lust-crazed version of her sweet, gentle voice, about how big and satisfying and adequate of a penis I have, smiling at me, feeling for me what I feel for her, then closing her eyes and riding out one of the screaming, squirting, squeezing, hair-bending five-minute orgasms that Rod Girder Productions claims as their unique selling point. That's what the Old Me used to fantasize about doing, as recently as earlier today.

And then, right after the Old Me finally achieved one frustrating little mouse-sneeze of an orgasm, but before he wiped himself clean and reactivated the card-key and unlocked the door of the Off-Line Backup Vault and returned to the Trouble Center; after the fantasy and the shame and the desire annihilated one another in their mutual impossibility, leaving a little puff of bitter smoke and burnt flesh at the spot in the Old Me's brain where rogue neurons of hope once dimly fired, but just before the Old Me trod a long circuit of shame back to my post in the Trouble Center, through the drink-snack-shuffleboard court, through the marketing-communications-weightlifting area, and past the ladies' room in the sad and perhaps creepy hope of accidentally bumping into Angela Fine, literally or figuratively, in the halls; between then and then, the Old Me used to shed exactly one and one-half tears from each eye, for a total of three.

The first tear was for myself, because I am so pathetic and small and weak and ashamed. I am also pale and pasty and scrawny, although better to be skeletally thin than morbidly obese like IT supervisor Gregg Lotz. But Gregg is shameless in his slovenly fat decrepitude—he slaps out a caffeine-driven disco rhythm on his breasts and thighs like a feisty manitee as he clomps down the halls, disgusting and terrifying the conspicuously fit and healthy non-IT employees of our international sportswear company—while the

10

Old Me knew far too well what his problems were, and struggled constantly to hide, to become invisible.

The second tear was for Angela Fine, because she is beautiful and pure and nice, and staples pictures of kittens to the pay envelopes of the entire IT department every Friday because she believes that little things count. If I were her lover I would be the most dedicated, kind, brave, understanding, sensitive lover any woman ever had. I would give her cunnilingus every morning, and fix her car, and rub her back and change all of the light bulbs in her house on a regular schedule before any of them ever actually burned out, and I would defend her home from thieves and her heart from loneliness and her body from violence and her laptop from viruses and unstable Microsoft updates. Because that is what a beautiful, perfect creature of Angela Fine's caliber—a caliber of one, a class unto herself—deserves.

But Angela Fine does not get what she deserves. Instead, Angela gets:

1. A brand-new pair of wide-rimmed glasses, slightly tinted —not nearly as flattering or sexy as the small, black-rimmed librarian glasses she used to wear, yet still gorgeous in context and incredibly lucky to be on her face—with which, aided by mascara, she disguises a swollen black eye; and
2. A small, perfectly round scab just beneath and behind her right ear, approximately eight millimeters in diameter, a kind of scab the Old Me knows well from his awful childhood; the kind of scab you get when your sadistic, abusive boyfriend or stepfather stabs you with a cigarette, as punishment.

(I am a keen observer in general, and a particularly keen observer of Angela Fine.)

The third tear is for my penis, with its Peter-Pan-like immunity to puberty; my withered disappointment, my runty pig, my tragic appendage. My third thumb. My problem.

It's late. After a relatively mild day of Trouble in the Trouble Center (87 tickets closed, 93 opened), my coworkers have gone home to their medium and large sized homes, to relationships based on mutual adequacy, and I have come here, to my secret sanctum in Retired Hardware Five, next to the loading dock, across from the lacrosse field. Retired Hardware Five is the mausoleum where we honor and dispose of our formerly beloved equipment, equipment that we could not live without until it was superseded by the even better equipment of the ever-encroaching digital future. Racked up on the walls all around me, lights unblinking, are 714 still hard disks that will never again spin, 220 dark monitors that will never again glow, 11,071 unplugged male and female ports—DB9, DB25, RJ45, 13W3, IEC, IDE, HPPI —that will never again feel the satisfying hookup of the cable-ends they were born to mate with. Many of them never even got the chance; dead virgins, gone to waste.

Spread before me on an empty server rack are the cardboard boxes I have downloaded, containing the crystallized essences of the New Me: the packets, the bottles, the instructions, the testimonials and the solutions to my MALE SEXUAL PROBLEMS.

The first cardboard box was shipped Priority 3-Day from the Cayman Islands by UPS. Inside, nestled in fresh and squeaky styrofoam peanuts, is a white plastic bottle of yellow pills labeled ENHANCEMENT PLACEBO FORMULA in a font that is discreet yet medically suggestive. This is MEGADIK—a proven herbal formula which complements the human growth hormone secreted by my pituitary gland. (If I even have a pituitary gland. My glands are a lifelong disappointment.) Dosage instructions are not included. I take three, and wash them down with Diet Fresca.

The second cardboard box, liberally stamped RUSH with smeary red ink, was shipped 2-Day Express by FedEx from the Cayman Islands. Inside, another small plastic bottle, very similar to the first, maybe even identical, containing similar yellow pills, one might even think the same yellow pills, but with a different label on the bottle, actually an only slightly different label, but just different enough for me to recognize it as a completely different male enhancement technology altogether: XtraHuge++, a naturally occurring erectile tissue conditioner from Korea. (Apparently they have huge dicks in Korea. Dicks bigger than their necks. Rod Girder did a special segment about Korean dicks in MONSTER COCKS WORLDWIDE. Rod Girder endorses XtraHuge++, as does his sometimes co-star Mitch Morecock.) The included instructions, in broken English, accompanied by gratuitous close-ups of some really extremely large, veiny penises entering the mouths of startled women, are clear. DOSAGE: ONE CAPSULE PER DAILY.

I take three capsules, and wash them down with Diet Fresca. My problems are immediate and severe.

The Internet knows all, and the Internet provides. Without eBay, I would have no polyvinyl Anime figurines. Without Google, I'd know nothing of Rod Girder, or the Monster Cocks cinematic cycle, or how to fix and deploy the complicated IT systems that our IT department must deploy and fix. And the Internet, in its kindness and wisdom, has been trying for years to grant me a larger, longer, thicker and more satisfying penis! But the Old Me wasn't ready, the Old Me fought the truth. The Old Me blocked and deleted those unsolicited offers before they hit my Inbox.

The Old Me, afraid of the truth, afraid to be free, afraid to be loved, employed an ever-evolving arsenal of anti-penis-enlargement tools: blacklists, graylists, SPF and MX records, honeypots, carefully honed lists of keywords like V|1gr@ and $e><ual and +ur6idid+y, ASCII insinuations of unspeakable acts ... unspeakable because they never happened to me, so why speak of them? The Old Me engineered and deployed a best-of-class mail-filtration system to purify the inbound and outbound

ones and zeroes of our international sportswear company network, to stem the rising tide of Internet sewage: realistic Rolex replicas, anonymous investment opportunities, cut-rate Canadian Cialis, weight-loss miracles, eternal youth, ultimate fighting power, and a million other excellent improvements to the sad, lonely life of an unloved Systems Administrator.

Every morning for four years three months and eleven days, the Old Me said no, and flushed away the Internet's fecal onslaught with one bitter keystroke. But today the New Me said YES.

In the third cardboard box, shipped Priority One by DHL from Moldova, is a ziplock bag, containing six smaller ziplock bags, each of which contains one day's pharmaceutically-impregnated WONDERCUM PLUS-PATCH. To achieve maximum results, I am to apply this patch to my penis, in the direction of preferred growth, before I go to sleep each night. As I sleep, my penis will busy itself with self-improvement, and in the morning I can remove it, or, optionally, move it to my scrotum and enjoy it for the rest of the workday. After six days, effects should be noticeable and pronounced, or I am entitled to request a full refund.

Oh, to be noticeable! Oh, to be pronounced! Oh, for Angela Fine to gaze upon me, not just in the chaste way she gazes upon kittens, hamsters, injured birds and members of the IT department, but in the hot, hungry, confused and ashamed way she gazes at the groin of that asshole who beats her.

That asshole with the monster cock—who she loves, instead of me—who beats her.

The Old Me denied an inescapable, ultimate human truth: the penis is the source of all male excellence! Strength, vigor, determination, chest hair and charisma flow outward from this central organ. Yes, it suppresses brain function somewhat, but I don't care. Until I have a larger, longer, thicker and more satisfying

penis, my love is useless torture! Angela Fine, perfect as she is, has
FEMALE SEXUAL PROBLEMS. She needs, craves, and I dare
say deserves a large, long, thick and satisfying penis. As a woman,
a sexual being, an earth goddess, this is her birthright and her
handicap. Women (I once denied but now admit) are hypnotized
by large concentrations of erectile tissue. They are drawn to them,
like moths to a light bulb. To ask otherwise of Angela would be
to misunderstand her beauty, and yet ... Angela's needs are so very
extreme, they could destroy her. Because the most satisfying penis
she has found, the penis whose orbit she is powerless to exit, is
mounted halfway down an abusive, mullet-wearing, coke-dealing,
Camaro-driving piece of Nazi surf-trash ... a man so dumb, his
name is actually Rock. A man so stupid and so evil that, given that
great gift that is the adoration and attention and body and sweet
love of Angela Fine, he does what with it? He beats her!

But I swear, with my hand upon the collected RFCs of
the Internet Engineering Task Force, that I will grow a better penis
for Angela, a perfect love penis of supernatural strength! And
when I'm coaxed forth from the desert of my loins this artificially-
irrigated wonder genital I will present it to her as a gift, a human
flower, a symbol and a token of my pure, undying, laser-like love.

Peering into my underpants, I apply two WONDERCUM
PLUS-PATCHES from box number three to my miserable third
thumb—one lengthwise, one across. Together, they envelop it
completely like a tiny tennis ball. Box number three mocks me.
Bring me box number four.

I'm not stupid. I know what "placebo" means. I have
taken six pills and applied two patches and I don't feel any larger
or any more satisfying. Boxes one through three are garbage, rip-
offs, trash. These patches on my penis offer only nicotine. I know
this, because the same Internet that gave them to me also gave
me the largest, longest-running and most satisfying online forum

15

for the Internet penis enlargement community: cocksmiths.com! Cocksmiths.com readers have tested MEGADIK and found no measurable enlargement. WONDERCUM, while causing some swelling of the testicles, produces less than 4 millimeters of increased manhood on average, well within statistical fluctuations. The jury is still out on XtraHuge++ (a mixture of Ephedra and horse semen) but early results are not promising. The Old Me spent perfectly good PayPal on this snake-oil, knowing it was snake oil, for the same reason the rest of the Cocksmiths.com readers did: we're all extremely desperate. There's no oil we won't rub on our sad little snakes.

But that was the Old Me. Inside box number four lies the New Me, waiting to uncoil and inflate. Box number four holds a new treatment—new like yesterday, bleeding edge, but very promising indeed. So promising, in fact, that this week the cocksmiths.com on-line forums are shuddering from the shock of the new, crumbling under gigabits of enthusiastic testimonial traffic and startling photographic evidence of the results from this new and promising treatment. The site has been knocked off-line three times this week. They're soliciting donations to pay for the added bandwidth consumed by the high-res, un-retouched before-and-after evidence. No one's sure what it is, or even where it comes from, but they're calling it the miracle we've waited for. They're calling it the cure.

They're saying it hurts. I don't care. Open the box. Peer inside. No pills, no patches, no suction pumps. It's a device, a sort of gun, steel and beige plastic, with a duck-billed maw on one end and a pistol grip on the other—plus a tenth-generation photocopy giving a single illustration of the device in use. The device doesn't even have a name, as such—it's available through a single non-English website with an unlisted IP address, shipped from somewhere in southeast Asia. But online, they're calling it the Monsterizer.

The Monsterizer implants, subcutaneously in the target

organ, a tiny gold pellet, which mysteriously Just Works. Just how it works we don't know yet, it's too new. The cocksmith. com forums, when not off-line, are abuzz with theories. Newbie members like dickcheney think it's a targeted hormonal release, some kind of steroid, but more experienced cock-smiths point out that those things have been tried and don't work except for side effects. Highly respected member goldenrod13 and some other old-timers have proposed it's a chip, RFID-style, talking to the penis and organizing its growth. Based on something they do in Iraq, with limbs, they say. Technology. And like all good technology, how it works doesn't matter unless it's broken. I don't need to know. It works by stimulation. Magnetism. Voodoo. I don't care. I peel back the patches, free up a parcel of my little peninsula ... pinch as much flesh as I can grip with the spring-loaded tongs ... close my eyes ... pull the trigger.

YES! IT! HURTS!

Wed Aug 06 11:10:05 PDT 2008:

Today is the first day of the rest of my penis! It's amazing, impossible, miraculous, uncomfortable. It's like painful swelling, basically. I'm running a slight fever and I itch like crazy. But user `goldenrod13` said the first day was like this for him. The first new day. User `small_paul` said the same thing. I've seen pictures of their dicks so I know I can trust them.

The Trouble Center is knee-deep in the following trouble this morning; aggravating WADSLAP breakdown in Shenzhou office kills trans-pacific virtual private network, delays final selection of Malaysian footwear shipment a scant two hours before some arbitrarily pre-determined summer fulfillment cutoff moment. Shenzhou office's hot-spare WADSLAP is mysteriously absent, probably embezzled. Upper-mid-sportswear-management shits their sportswear, demands immediate solutions to impossible problems: blood, sweat, spit, bailing wire, bales of cash, helicopters full of replacement WADSLAP air-dropped over Shenzhou, time travel, human blood, whatever we've got. Just Do It.

While IT panic builds, I calmly peruse the logs. A bitter intercontinental spat has broken out between the two WADSLAPs, concerning whose turn it is to shift the transmission window. Shenzhou calls Virgina "out of sync". Virgina calls Shenzhou "non-compliant." Every seventeen seconds they scream at each other, break up, re-train, bicker, scream some more. While Gregg Lotz oozes the pale gelatin sweat of stress and barks through the phone at Shenzhou in a pidgin of swearwords and TLAs which we both know Shenzhou doesn't grok, and the NetOps grunts and the Chad Squad try desperately to look busy, and upper-mid-management sharpens their axes outside the Trouble Center doors, your humble sysadmin:

1. quietly determines that the WADSLAP manufacturer released a patch this morning,
2. theorizes that Shenzhou may have promptly installed that patch, particularly after last week's pidgin & TLA tirade from Gregg Lotz re: prompt patch installation,
3. remote-installs the same patch on the matching WADSLAP in Virginia, and reboots.

Instantly, the warring WADSLAPs come to their senses, renew their marital vows and engage in immediate hot data coitus. Several hundred iterations of the same footwear order march in single file across the virtual private urethra of their love, and fifteen minutes later it's Shenzhou's problem.

I did that! With my new penis! The Old Me would have panicked, hidden, perhaps wept when mid-upper-sportswear-manager Phil Tong burst into the Trouble Center, his morning coffee running down his tie, clutching an ink-stained printout, calling the IT department 'clueless trolls' and dialing our manager's manager's manager on his iPhone. The new me didn't even blink.

Phil Tong, I'm guessing, has a very small penis. Not as small as mine, but smaller than most. I know this because I know what kind of pornography he downloads. We have the same tastes.

Phil Tong is always bitching about IT, decrying the competence in IT, demanding IT heads on mid-upper-sportswear-management platters. He needs to feel large, larger than someone else. IT fills this role for him. We are a department of the kinds of people who fill that role. Gregg Lotz, Chad Day, Chad Wankel, Grunt Number One and Grunt Number Two: misfits, nerds, social failures, Information Technology professionals. We wipe the asses of machines so we won't have to talk to people. Phil Tong threatens us because we don't fight back.

Thirty-seven minutes and fifteen seconds ago, I scooped up a virulent sample of child pornography from the external spam-stream and installed it on Phil Tong's laptop. For eleven minutes and thrity-three seconds I strategized how best to anonymously notify Human Resources of how Phil uses company hardware to pursue his dangerous perversion, but then I relented. My new penis is a forgiving penis. One day it will crush Phil Tong's penis, but for now, let them live together in peace. For now, let Gregg Lotz issue a technical debriefing to a grateful but still panicky boardroom, while I visit the executive soccer/rugby changing booth, for the third time today, to adore my beautiful new penis in the full-length mirror.

Wed Aug 06 12:23:40 PDT 2008:

Hello, little monster. I swear you're bigger than you were two hours ago. Once you were a thumb, now you are a fat big toe, long and red and laced with busy veins, a toe to kick someone's ass with. Right where your knuckle would be is a hot white raised bump, where the subcutaneous golden seed works its magic. Your fingertip is a swelling, hot red bulb—a rare desert flower now blooming for the first time in thirty years.

Rooted beneath your soft, curly undergrowth ... is Jack Stalker, a guy who needs to get a grip. This could all go wrong, Jack. This could be a localized infection disguised as male enhancement. A crippling injury, a rip-off. If that happens ... you will want to kill yourself, Jack. It will be the straw that broke the tiny camel. Only, if that happens, you won't have the nerve. Because then The Old Me will be back, and he'll just dig a sub-basement in the basement of his soul, carry his things downstairs, and cry a few more tears.

Only I can kill the Old Me.

Phil Tong is waiting outside the executive soccer/rugby changing booth. He glares disapprovingly at me. I know, and he knows, that this booth is reserved for executive changing. But he knows, and I know, that sysadmins are everywhere always, scurrying underfoot or suspended overhead, pulling wires, testing hookups, installing repeaters and base stations and HVAC and AC and whatever other technology is necessary for executive changing in the digital age. Making things work. Phil Tong and his management ilk need us to do these things, though they hate that they do.

"What's the story, Jack?" demands Phil Tong impatiently. "Stalking someone?" He puts two fingers against his temple to massage the constant headache that I and my coworkers give him.

"I'm done. Just tying down some D-Links. It's all yours."

"D-Links?"

"Yes. In the crawlspace. They were dangling."

"Is that what you do all day?" he snidely demands, surely expecting me to whimper or run away. I do neither. In truth, Phil Tong hasn't a clue what we do all day, doesn't know what a D-Link is, so I could say yes or no or "one, one, zero, zero," and it would all be rot13 to him. But before I can deliver more than a shrug, he rolls his eyes, shoves past me and shuts the door.

I see he brought along his laptop. I don't think he's here for soccer/rugby.

Wed Aug 06 20:15:40 PDT 2008:

I wasn't even trying to bump into Angela today. (I wouldn't have been holding a Diet Fresca, obviously, if I'd been trying to bump into her.) I've been preoccupied, busy ... I was on my way to kick the printer in receivables—every day before 16:00 PDT it must be kicked, squarely, in the side, for historical reasons—and it was 15:42 PDT already and I had lost track of time in the cocksmiths.com chat rooms, exchanging my first excited reports with a group of disbelieving noobs, who called me a bullshitter and demanded photographs of my penis in a way

21

I found slightly invasive, and then actually receiving a private chat request from `goldenrod13` himself (!!!) at 3:57pm PDT, which is, in the context of cocksmiths.com, a kind-of-big deal, when suddenly my phone buzzed to remind me that it had buzzed twice earlier to remind me to kick the printer in receivables before `16:00 PDT`, and it was already `15:58 PDT`. So I switched my chat mode from "Available" (icon: large erect penis with bow tie) to "Be Right Back" (icon: droopy penis next to cigarette), and headed towards Receivables at a trot.

Passing the drink-snack-shuffleboard court I felt thirsty, dry and hot—as I've felt all day—so I grabbed a quick Diet Fresca as my phone buzzed a more insistent, throbbing vibration to inform me it was already `16:00 PDT` and I had better move it. And the friction of my jeans as I ran towards Receivables with the drink in my hand, plus the itching of my new penis, plus the vibration of the phone in my pocket, suddenly it all at once started to well up and grip me in a crazy combined feeling of well-being and energy and strength, and I just ran, faster, and felt it surging stronger, and I closed my eyes and turned the corner and crashed right into Angela Fine as electricity gripped my knees and strange, hot juice erupted into my underwear, as I spilled diet Fresca all over her and her paperwork as she spilled paperwork and coffee all over me and my penis, as we tumbled to the floor together in one glorious, disgusting, humiliating pile-up of orgasm and shame.

And then, up out of the ashes of yesterday rose the Old Me, supplicant and sniveling. Oh God, I am such a stupid nothing. Oh God, Angela Fine thinks I'm such a loser. Oh God, her hair smells like a beautiful, ripe peach. Oh God, she's staring at me, oh God, that is some extremely hot painful coffee. Don't look at my crotch! No, please look! I can see her bra! I'm a pervert! It's pink! I'm an idiot! Did we just have sex? Am I on fire? This pleasure, this pain ...

Angela Fine grasped my shoulders as we struggled to our feet together, diet Fresca dripping off her wide-rimmed glasses.

She stared, with great concern and concentration, directly at the site where my large, long, thick, satisfying penis will soon spring forth for her.

"Oh gosh, Jack, are you okay? I'm so sorry! I don' t know how I did that!"

"No no no! It's me, I'm sorry, I'm stupid. I was, there's—oww! Hi!"

"Oh no!" She bit her finger in concern. "Go pour some water on it!"

"No, I gotta go kick the printer. It's okay, I'm hot. You're hot too. Hi Angela!"

"Jack, this could be serious! Like that lady at McDonalds!" Her face a perfect circle of sweetness and worry, and right then and there I fell in love with her a second time, superimposed on the love I already fell, double down. All the world's goodness shines out of Angela Fine's brown eyes. "I'm just so sorry!" she said.

"I gotta go!" I said. "Will you talk to me some more when I'm not burning?"

"Jack, please be okay!"

"Going! Sorry! Bye!"

And the Old Me hauled ass right out of there, ran all the way back to Retired Hardware Five in shame, and disrobed to find my poor, guilty-looking new penis, head hung low, bashfully awaiting punishment like a little pot-bellied piglet who's wet the carpet.

I cradled it in my hand. Warm, soft, pulsing with the beat of my own heart. A naked mole-rat caught above ground, defenseless and confused. How could I stay angry at that precious little life, staring at me with its hamster eye, trembling in shame. My own penis. Fruit of my loins! I used to hate you. Will you forgive me? Can we start over?

I decided then and there to call it Lassie.

I changed into my other pair of pants, dirty but at least

not sticky, and walked jauntily back to Building One, mentally re-living that anxious, intoxicating moment over and over: that hot instant of the smell of her and the heat from inside me, inside Lassie, and the aroma of diet Fresca and coffee and photocopies and Angela Fine staring at my crotch. It makes my knees weak, even now, just thinking of it. Oh, Angela!

And then I returned to the Trouble Center with my head in a cloud of Trojan Condom advertisements ... and caught hell from Gregg Lotz, passing along the hell he caught from Receivables, for not having kicked the printer.

Therefore: now it is 20:43 PDT and Lassie and I are on month-end tape swap duty in Ice Station Zebra, the climatized server room in building six, as punishment, subbing for NetOps grunt number one so he can go do something at eight. The rest of IT has gone home. Wrapped in the official IT parka for this room, I pull a backup tape out of the jukebox, hand-label it with an anti-static pen, and plunge a fresh tape in the open slot of the Xebnix tape carousel, slowly, gently, lovingly. I do that one hundred and forty four times, and every time the tape transport swallows my offering I think of Angela.

The second seed is planted. goldenrod13 says I must be careful. He says there's such a thing as too much. For him that may be true. But my problems are immediate, and severe. The Old Me must die so that Lassie can live.

Thu Aug 07 09:08:07 PDT 2008:

Yes! Yes! Yes!

This is the most amazing thing that has ever happened to me. This is better than every Rod Girder film combined, and it's real! Lassie woke me up this morning, squirming, tapping, wriggling me awake. He's already five and one thirty-second inches long, and almost four and three quarters inches in circumference! That's literally twice as long as he was two days ago! At this growth rate my penis will be ten inches long in three more days! After that .. I don't know, that would be more than enough to show to Angela. This, frankly, is already more than I've ever dreamed of. The Monsterizer is real! It works! I'm sorry I ever doubted you, Monsterizer! Lassie, I love you.

Lassie's burning has subsided, although the itching remains severe. I can touch him now. In fact I can't stop touching him! He really is like a rambunctious puppy, so excited and full of energy. This is what a penis is supposed to feel like! Finally we are together, a boy and his penis, exploring the world! I've been showing Lassie new places all day: a loaf of bread (soft, crumbly), a jar of peanut butter (exciting, messy), a cup of diet Fresca (cold, sticky), the hot-swappable drive bay of a Hewlett Packard RL3000 information server (shocking!) So many places exist for a penis to go, if that penis is just long enough to reach. A beautiful new world of crevices and caverns.

The Monsterizer, I predict, will change human civilization forever! Computers are nothing compared to this. Rural electrification, running water and sliced bread are nothing. I declare small penises extinct! Nobody with a credit card and

25

Internet access need ever experience smallness or inadequacy again. All men shall be giants! A new era of peace and genital pride dawns worldwide as we put aside our petty squabbles, shed our insecurity, and hump our way to global understanding! I'm awed to participate in this pivotal moment in human evolution, an early settler on a rich new continent forested with large, long, thick, satisfying penises.

Lassie years to run free. Every time I pass a female employee in the halls, Lassie twitches at his leash. Young, old, married, fat, Lassie doesn't care. What a nut! It's a big responsibility, raising a monster cock, teaching it right from wrong. Women have no idea.

Or maybe that's not true: one visual merchandiser, a red-headed older woman named Wendy, brushed past me in the Hall of Sports Heroes And Photocopying, and Lassie nearly jumped out and bit her.

And she looked. I saw her look. And I think I saw her smile.

Thu Aug 07 19:44:23 PDT 2008:

Today the Trouble Center was hip-deep in the following kinds of trouble: The east coast is seized with mass hysteria due to a wave of unexplained killings. Virginia state sheriffs are soliciting tips from the Internet. The Internet is flooding their on-line tip-server with tips, and by sad coincidence our Virginia BGP box is co-located not only with their tip-server but also with a major CNN.com news mirror; ergo, the fiber into that co-lo is hosebagged by hysterical suburbanites finking on their mailmen, and only a spluttery dribble of ones and zeroes remains for the other co-lo residents, including our international sportswear company's newly launched yoga-and-breakdancewear online store for single urban mothers. Ergo, urban sports product manager Phil Tong is livid. (What else is new?) Dollars, he says, are dropping on the floor in Virginia, and we in IT, he says, have our heads up our asses.

And also: today the Internet caught a cold. Spam and virus counts just doubled, overnight, everywhere. That's both scary and amazing—it's as if every asshole in the world suddenly sprouted a second asshole. Some new cabal of sleazy `h@xx0rs` has announced their arrival, some shift in the Russian cybermafia power structure has admitted fresh players to the game of viruses and spam, and they are busy, busy beavers. Everything is slow. Everything is late. Many things are offline—cocksmiths.com, for example, but also our main corporate Web site and two of our main B2B sites—but they'll come back when the storm passes. My spam filter is holding. The firewall is solid.

And also: the Hewlett Packard RL3000 Information Server is down. Information Receiving is hot for information, but Information Services can't get it up. Information Receiving demands a vendor tech on site within the hour, and I don't think I want to be around when he gets here. (Silly Lassie!)

And more: backhoes, dead drives, interruptions in the Uninterruptible Power Supply, managers who cannot grasp a spreadsheet no matter how wide it is spread. Trouble, trouble, trouble. Solve, solve, solve. 72 tickets closed today, 137 opened. It never ends. As long as there are things and idiots, idiots will break things.

But I don't mind, and neither does Lassie. We've got each other, and we've got the future. Stiff black hair is sprouting on my chest, I feel my pores clearing, I feel my voice deepening, my mane thickening. Energy and power and strength are coursing through me. I grow studly!

Is it normal for a penis to jump around so much? Lassie is so enthusiastic! It reminds me of a time when I was little, visiting my cousin Sam in Eau Claire, Wisconsin, when Sam's pet ferret Mister Bonzo climbed up my leg and ran around in my pants. That's what I keep mistaking this for, whenever Lassie starts twitching like this. Mister Bonzo the ferret bit my penis, but if he tried that today he'd have a fight on his hands. You have Mister

Bonzo outclassed, don't you Lassie? You little monster!

Tonight, in my secret sanctum, surrounded by my polyvinyl figurine collection and my Xbox and my movies, Lassie and I are posing for photographs, to show all our friends at cocksmiths. com what we're up to. Six inches! That's an inch longer than this morning! And as I struggle with lighting and focus and finding the right pile of de-commissioned hardware to bring the camera to loin height, I am posing, in my mind, not for the obnoxious, nay-saying, possibly gay noobs on the forums, but for my princess, my perfect love.

Angela, Angela, Angela Fine. Lassie and I will make you mine.

Fri Aug 08 08:09:10 PDT 2008:

Angela, Angela, Angela Fine: Lassie and I will hunt down the abusive bad news cokehead surf-Nazi who dares to call you 'sweet-cheeks' and shove his own cock down his throat!

Why do you go back to him, Angela? Why do you allow him to debase you? Is a larger, longer, thicker, more satisfying penis really worth the pain?

I am a keen observer of you, Angela. From my window in the Trouble Center I observed you in the Field Of Dreams And Parking this morning, dropped off by your concerned girlfriend Estrella after a brief but tender hug, and I observed you limping, just slightly, with your head hung low and your tender hand touching a tender spot on your side, as you limped through the entrance and on up to your second floor desk, there to staple pictures of kittens to our pay envelopes in pain, and draw smiley faces on our Friday Party notices in pain, and brighten our workplace with the smile that hides your pain.

Fury! Aggression! Black feelings the Old Me and his three thumbs never knew are pumping through the New Me like hot poison! Lassie turned nine today, incidentally. Nine inches of seething hatred for that bastard asshole who's named after Earth's stupidest material. Lassie's two white eyes squint angrily when I take him out for lotion. His happy-go-lucky personality is gone today, Angela. Today, Lassie wants blood!

Fri Aug 08 08:09:10 PDT 2008:
Today the Trouble Center weathered the following shit-storm of trouble: general utter total breakdown of everything

29

Internetty and/or located on the entire east coast! All last night, heaping boatloads of spam throttled everybody—particularly, interestingly, yet unfortunately including some newly deployed ConEd electricity futures trading bullshit system, triggering a truly stupid and preventable over-delivery of megawatts at major crossover points in the eastern seaboard's electrical grids, and boom: PCB-laden shrapnel rains down from telephone poles all up and down the east coast. Blackout! Three of the four major Internet handshake centers go dark just like that, their redundant power is up but the telcos that feed them are down. Gaping holes in Blackberry coverage, so upper-management can't even call to complain. All because of spam! Plus: killers run loose in the streets, uncaught still.

Meanwhile, here on the west coast: overloads, under-supplies, and an onslaught of refugee data from Virginia. Everything distributed must now be consolidated, here. Ice Station Zebra is close to boiling, and business-crazed couriers fresh from private jets keep bursting in here, demanding uploads to Shenzhou. Shenzhou claims everything is fine but nobody believes them. Tickets and tickets and tickets of Trouble flutter down from on high. Gregg Lotz exudes the odor of the damned, and dutifully conveys to us the screaming babble of a terrified upper management. The Chad Squad builds up emergency flotation devices from hot spares, as Grunts One and Two jury-rig a refugee data center in the Footwear History Library, as I re-route configurations and re-configure routers until my fingertips are numb, and I suddenly remember that none of this compares to you.

Meanwhile, the rest of the company decided it was time for Friday Party. That's where I found you, Angela Fine: by the outdoor bungee and picnic tower where our international sportswear company division throws itself the same party every fourteen days. The mood was nervous, habitual, bleakly festive. Sportswear professionals picked at high-fiber hors d'oeuvres, or dangled tentatively from the Bungee Mesa, or warded off the shock of the crazy news with light beer and cheap jokes. You sat alone on a bench, smiling absently, staring out into the parking lot with a look on your face that even I, keen observer, could not fathom. You nibbled on a carrot stick in a way that ties Lassie in knots, and twisted fretfully at the cap of your non-twist-cap beer.

I opened that beer for you, Angela, with my trusty pocket tool, as I would open for you all beers, all boxes, all bags of chips, all cartons of milk, all doors, all windows, my savings account, my checking account, my mint-condition polyvinyl anime figurines, my heart, my soul, the fly of my trousers, everything I have, for you, if you would just let me. I opened your beer, and handed it to you, and spoke my most heroic word:

"Fixed."

"Oh, Jack! I'm—" was your three word reply ...

... before the HORRIBLE NOISE. The wretched, bastard cancellation of all other sounds, the primal metallic GRUNT of the over-sized air horn of the rectal-black Camaro of the square-headed, cop-mustached, muscle-T-wearing surf-Nazi coke dealer who beats you, who honks at you from the Field Of Dreams And Parking and beats you, who yells "Hey sweet-cheeks! Let's move it huh?" and HONKS his horn at you again, HONKS HONKS HONKS his horn at you, in front of your entire department ... and who also, let us not forget, beats you.

I observed you keenly. I watched your mind parse his dial-tone, in discrete procedural steps:

```
If A(ngela),
        then B(oyfriend);

If B(oyfriend), then {
        C(ock),
        C(ruelty),
        C(amaro)
    }.
```

"Have a nice weekend, Jack," are the other five things you said to me in your desperately cheerful voice as you gathered up your purse and put down your beer and walked out into the parking lot of your ongoing abuse and boarded the muscle car of your destruction.

I screamed, but you didn't hear me. You heard tires squealing and jock-rock blaring from the stereo. I threw the rest of your beer at that Camaro, but you didn't see the foamy broken glass. It didn't reach you ... I throw like a girl.

I tried to chase you, but was restrained by the Chad Squad:

"Jack Jack hey! Hey Jack! Woah Jack. Don't crash."

I couldn't form words, only angry moans and spittle in my throat, as a cloud of uncombusted Camaro exhaust blew back over me like piss.

"You're crashing, Jack. Reboot!" pleaded Chad D.

"Here, eat chips," begged Chad W. "Salty goodness! Drink Fresca ... stabilize ... stabilize ..."

Chad and Chad sat me down and fed me and watched me and held my hand, addressing my malfunction, while the iron bands of hatred around my head and my penis slowly loosened and fell away.

"Sorry ... sorry guys ... inappropriate freak-out, sorry."

"Fuck of a day, man," said Chad D. "Too many tickets. Too much trouble."

Sat Aug 09 00:23:11 PDT 2008:
We stayed late, cleaning up the mess, dumping the files, flushing the routes, stabilizing the patient. The patient will live. The Internet, I'm not so sure. This is the Worst Storm Ever, easily, but all over the world, sysadmins and NOC workers, IT professionals all, are laying hands upon the Internet, massaging it, keeping it up. The porn, as we say, must flow.

Today, sixty-one percent of legitimate Internet traffic is pornography. That's just the pornographers who pay their bills and attend trade conferences and have customer relations managers. Their explicit depictions of sexual acts are legitimate, solicited traffic. To a significant degree, pornography subsidizes all other Internet packets. But as of today legitimate, solicited traffic is down to just over thirty-one percent of overall packets. The rest is spam.

At the climax of the twentieth century, humankind pooled billions of dollars and millions of hours of genius-engineer-sweat, in an unprecedented spirit of cooperation and market freedom, to create the capstone of human progress we call the Internet: a vast intelligent self-healing network of digitized ideas, speaking directly to all mankind, connecting us all to one another at the speed of thought ... and the Internet, in gratitude, constantly and tactlessly urges all humankind to enlarge its penises, enhance its breasts, lose its unsightly fat, attach vibrating pleasure toys to its genitals, ingest all kinds of drugs, and gaze endlessly into its bottomless pool of explicit multimedia pan-sexual exploitation, the greatest horde of pornography that has ever existed.

Maybe the Internet is hot for us. Maybe it wants our monster cocks.

I got home sometime after midnight. Chad and Chad offered to give me a lift; It was hard to convince them I'd rather ride my bicycle. I took a long shower at the Mark Spitz pool/sauna/conference cluster, waiting for them to give up on me. When I came out I didn't see them, but to be safe I got on my bike and rode out Victory Drive, down Victory Circle, left on Victory Expressway, left on Sportsmanship Boulevard, up the unused multi-use path, and back to Retired Hardware Five, where I slipped through the deactivated fire exit, unseen.

I live at work. Why not? Work is my life. Retired Hardware Five is storage enough for me, my movies, my collections. And my

Lassie. Lassie is happy here, I think. It's a dark, quiet place, just like my pants. And all this retired hardware, that once blinked and beeped and toiled for us, and told us everything it knew ... I don't know, I just feel it deserves to be remembered. Kept company. Honored, somehow. I still find it beautiful.

I used to have an apartment, but I never went there. And then I got a little too over-extended into polyvinyl figurines, a bit maxed-out ... I stopped paying the rent and I stopped going home, and life has hardly changed in the six months since.

I'm burnt out. Today's anger and hatred and tension are just a few loose embers knocking around in the ash-pit of my heart. I want sleep ... but Lassie won't let me. Lassie wants to play.

I can't, I protest. But Lassie insists. Poor Lassie ...

Okay. I haven't watched Monster Cocks Six in a while. I cue up the DVD in my trusty lap-mate, stretch out on my squeaky styro-peanut beanbag bed, and release my pet from his cage ...

Lassie! You startled me, you're so huge! You've been busy! You're really on your way to Monster Cock status! Rod Girder would be proud of you! So heavy, so thick... how long? Eleven? No! That can't be right ... eleven! That's enormous! The implications ... I'm reeling! I think you've made it into the top tenth, the top twentieth maybe, of all penis measurements worldwide. I really wish cocksmiths.com would come back up. People need to meet you! You need to come out and shine.

Menu screen. Flying logo. Credits. Fade in ... I'm Rod Girder, welcome to my world ... blah blah blah, asses, a swimming pool, more blah blah blah, Lana Liason raises an eyebrow, a brief attempt at acting as she slips off Rod's loose-fitting trousers and gets slapped in the face by his half-hard meat. Suck suck suck, etc ... yawn. Lana Liason is slightly cross-eyed. She's a big fake. She bleaches her eyebrows in a way that's so slutty it's revolting. She looks nothing like Angela Fine. No porn star comes close.

I start to rub some lotion on Lassie anyway, but he rears up and wriggles away from me, peering at me with his two little white eyes. Sometimes he looks like a real snake, a scary cobra ... but he's not scary, he's my Lassie. C'mere, Lassie. You like this stuff, it soothes the itch.

Lassie doesn't want that. Lassie wants something else.

What is it, Lassie? What's the trouble? What do you want?

No.

Sorry Lassie, no. No Monsterizer tonight.

Lassie, listen to me: you are *so* big. Epic, you are! And growing, still! I'm proud of you, but frankly, I don' t know how much more you're going to grow even without another monsterization. I've been thinking about this, and I've decided ... we need to wait, Lassie.

Oh fucking hell, Lassie. Stop doing this to me. I said no. What is sexy about the Monsterizer? The Monsterizer *hurts*, Lassie. It makes you red and itchy. You don't want that. I don't want that. I don't want ... Lassie, please ...

You know ... come to think of it ... yes, I do want it. I want it really severely and immediately. In fact, I have absolutely, positively, one-hundred-per-cent for sure got to stick my BIG new COCK in that Monsterizer this FUCKING minute! Right now, oh yeah, oh baby, it's ON!

Rod Girder is flipping Lana Liason over on the poolside recliner, and I'm tearing through the disorganized debris on the concrete floor by my beanbag ... where is it? Shit! Where did I put it? Where's the Monsterizer? Oh shit, shit, shit ...

What's that, Lassie? Where are you pointing? Under the bean bag ... yes! The fucking MONSTERIZER! Good boy! C'mere, baby ... oh God I NEED to feel my Lassie in the cold hard metal jaws of that thing, yes! Its plastic pistol GRIP, oh yeah, it's a tight squeeze, OW, because we're so BIG, OW, yeah, OW, yeah, the TEETH! OW, OW, OW ... it's coming,

Lassie, hang on, here it comes ... NOW!

I pull the trigger, the Monsterizer sinks its fang deep into Lassie's neck, and all at once: cuntfulls, assfulls, mouthfulls, Angelafulls of semen come screaming out of me, my testicles shuddering, my ass kicking space, Lassie spitting and spitting semen in giant arcs across the room, pink semen, all over my Lapmate, my bean-bag, my polyvinyl figurines, my Xbox, everything covered in pink semen, FUCK! Come on, Lassie! Come ON! Lassie writhes, twitches, and spits, FUCK! My spine, my feet, my mind, still coming, still pumping, yards of semen, quarts of semen, pints of red semen ... Oh! Ride it, Lassie! Squeeze it! Push it! Good boy, Lassie! Don't stop! Don't let it go! I'm spinning, I'm falling, I'm floating, I'm coming, I'm bleeding, oh God, bloody red semen, all over me, yes! I'm passing out, I'm dying, I'm dying so good ... oh, Lassie ... oh dear ... I never knew ... it could be ... so fucking good ... keep going, Lassie ... run ... get Angela ... get help ...

Mon Aug 11 06:23:40 PDT 2008:

Update: that *so* never happened. Absolutely did not happen. Bad dream. I don't know what happened Friday night but it wasn't that. Something, though, something happened. While I slept all weekend long, something crawled into Retired Hardware Five and killed and ate some other thing. Racoons? Maybe ... gore on the floor, slime on the ceiling, bloody tracks leading all over the place, Jesus ... well, it was dark when I left. Maybe it's not so bad in the light. Maybe.

One of the many advantages of living in Retired Hardware Five was not needing to clean. But now ... well, this just means that it's even more urgent that Angela and I get together, that I tell her how I feel, that I show her what I've got to offer, that she see the clear logic and beauty of choosing me over that stone-headed dickweed in the black Camaro, and that we eventually find a nice apartment together.

Only ... I crept across campus at dawn and made it here to the showers without being seen, to wash away the gore and scum and whatever. But now, here I am, faced with a large, new, unexpected SEXUAL PROBLEM.

Large as in vast. Containing multitudes.

It never occurred to me before, but there must be certain hardships in the glamorous porn-star life of Rod Girder. Issues of tailoring, for instance. Difficulty bending over. A light-headedness when a limited supply of blood rushes downward, away from the brain. Discomfort in chairs. And ... I don't know if Ron Girder has this particular problem, but: it just won't sit still. It won't stop jumping around, writhing like a snake. It's agitated.

37

Sit, Lassie. Heel!

Lassie won't sit or heel. Lassie won't stop thrashing around. He has three angry eyes and he's big as my forearm. It takes two hands to pin him down.

Absolutely no more Monsterizer for you! No more. None. This is enough. This is plenty of monster. Beyond satisfying. Lassie, I love you but you've got to start watching your weight. I'm sure that once we lay off the device for a few days, you will quit freaking out and start getting with the program. We have an important mission, Lassie. You mustn't act like this around Angela!

It's a cable management problem, really. I always carry a few spare velcro straps and some zip ties to keep unruly cables from tripping me up. The Trouble Center runs a tight ship. Lassie, I'm sorry but you're being very bad, and I need to get to work, I don't have time for this. I'll make it up to you, I promise. Please, Lassie, quit struggling!

It's Monday, so I have clean clothes. Underwear, though, is just not happening. (Ron Girder never wears underwear either. I can get used to that.) Parachute pants will have to do, and a black company tee with the ISC logo on the reverse, and on the obverse our corporate motto: Just Do It. And a struggling, squirming penis strapped tightly, painfully, to my right leg.

This can't be right. I mean, it's great—I dreamed of this, I need this, I love my Lassie, I just ... I need to talk to `goldenrod13`, `small_paul`, `mosquitoboy`, any of them. The elder cocksmiths, those farther along the path than I. Cocksmiths.com, I need you!

Mon Aug 11 13:23:40 PDT 2008:

Good Christ! Today the Trouble Center snorkles in the following biblical flood of Trouble: the East Coast and much of the Midwest now enjoy what the President refuses to call "martial law," as power stations continue to explode and everything even

38

remotely attached to the Internet goes absolutely batshit. TV is dark, cell phones are dark, rumors are rampant. One internet-simulcasting radio station situated right on top of a hydroelectric dam on a river in upstate New York is managing to calm everybody down over there by reporting, as fact, the comforting rumor that an organized gang of serial killers is raping and stabbing and smashing its way from Newport to Miami. The Army and the National Guard and even the INS are busy securing the interstates and shooting people by accident and generally whipping up the panic level, setting up checkpoints from Minnesota to Texas and marching slowly eastward to figure out what the fuck, if anything the fuck, is happening. IMAO, information junkies nationwide, sick without their fix, are going through some bad cold turkey, clearly, and seeing shit that isn't real. People on the east coast do not know how to relax. It's utterly stupid.

Here in Trouble Central, we are urgently but methodically cauterizing the stumps of our network, backing up our most crucial ones and zeroes, and groping through the mudslide of spam for solid servers that respond to pings. Amazingly, a few legit packets still flow across the network and back. Sysadmins worldwide are falling back to UUCP, BBSes and pinging in morse code. (Geriatric FIDONET users, all four of them, wag their fingers at the Internet and, I assume, exchange smug notes about how right they were all along.) Mid-upper-management has given up on spring sportswear shipments, projections, tracking, accounting, given up on accomplishing any actual things at all, and wants only information. Unsuccessful probing suggests our German competition is equally bogged down in equally thick data quicksand, and mid-upper-management finds this somehow comforting. Shenzhou, when online, insists everything is fine and under control with such vehemence that we assume they are smoking opium—we've caught them doing that before.

Phil Tong thinks it's a virus. Phil Tong barges into Trouble Center with a crazed look in his eye and insists it's a virus, a virus, it's got to be a virus, demands to know if we morons have even considered the possibility that it might be a virus, and if not why not? The Chad Squad, ever vigilant, jumps on Gregg Lotz and restrains him before Gregg can jump on Phil Tong and strangle him by his coffee-stained tie. Phil Tong warns us not to touch him and lurches away, limping.

Users think everything is a virus. Yes, sure, that's part of it, self-replicating spam-bots are part of the Spamscape, have been for years. But they've never had this kind of traction. Somebody fucked up somewhere, some major door was left unlocked, left wide open, and in flowed the slime. Somewhere in Estonia, pimply pre-teen uberhackers are giggling and high-fiving each other. Won't somebody please shoot them?

Meanwhile: Chad D. and Chad W. are fucking heroes! The same stress that's driving Phil Tong to nervous breakdown only makes these guys work harder, think clearer, do more. No complains, no freakouts, they just keep hacking through the tickets like spartans on the battlefield. Outside this office a shit-storm of mad trouble is sweeping west, but the troubles of IT are rational and we will fix them, ticket by ticket. This trouble keep us sane.

Our firewall is under constant attack on all channels. All known weaknesses of its OS and the OS it masquerades as are probed on all protocols: IP4, IP6, ATM; BGP forgeries, timing attacks, brute force token storms, SNMP probes. The mail daemon is hammered senseless by wave upon crashing pungent wave of spam which leave it stammering: ELHO? QUIT! ELHO? But the bulkheads are holding. The patches are watertight. The ship will not sink. And if I lash myself to the mast, I can send out signals on the open sea.

Mon Aug 11 23:23:40 PDT 2008:
It's very late. I'm in my corner cube, taking a break ... sending out an SOS to 8.231.11.22 .

Ping? Ack? Knock knock? Hello? I knock 100 times on

their front door ... three pings come back.

Their website is down, their mail gateway is down, but cocksmiths.com is not dead yet. I telnet to the quickchat port as I rummage through my memory for the format of this fairly stupid yet mysteriously popular chat dialect. Slow as molasses my packets march across the battlefield, arriving truncated and misaligned. Slow as glaciers, the reply advances back across the carnage. The remote qchat daemon asks:

```
001 YES?
200 USER goldenrod13 QCHAT_REQ(l=10): its
2 big.
.... 301 BUMMER: USER NOT AVAILABLE.
200   USER  small_paul  QCHAT_REQ(l=28):
everythings going major nuts.
.... 301 BUMMER: USER NOT AVAILABLE.
200   USER  mosquitoboy  QCHAT_REQ(l=17):
wheres everybody?
.... 302 HARSH: REQUEST DENIED.
200   USER  mosquitoboy  QCHAT_REQ(l=102):
hello? help me! its getting bigger & its getting
inside my mind! How do I stop? Did this happen
to you?
.... 302 HARSH: REQUEST DENIED.
200USERmosquitoboyQCHAT_REQ(l=28;pri=1):
MB: is it inside your mind 2?
.... 666 BOGUS: CHAT TERMINATED.
```

"Hey Jack?"

Chad D. pokes his round head into my square workspace with his worry face on. He looks like caffeine death, all pale and twitchy and his meager supply of hair sticking out sideways. I can't imagine how I must look. But that's how the world looks today.

"Jack, there's some dudes here ..."

Chad indicates behind him with his thumb, where stands a tall, grey-haired man in baggy black clothes, looking at me like I'm some kind of bug. A note-pad sticks out of the lapel pocket of his jacket. Behind him stand two cops—a bald one and a young one —and behind the two cops stands Gregg Lotz, mouth opening and closing but no words coming out, and three campus security guards, dumb & zealous, ready to assist with any insecurity that two cops and a police detective can't handle.

"Hi, mister, um ... Stalker? Can I call you Jack?"

I nod.

He smiles like a used-car salesman and speaks to me slowly, clearly, just in case I am retarded: "Thank you. My name's Malcolm Dean, I'm a police detective." He extends a cautious handshake request. "I'm sorry to interrupt you, I know everybody's up to their neck in problems today ..."

"Friday."

He raises an eyebrow. "Friday?"

"Friday was my neck. Today's deeper."

"Is it?" He glances to the bald cop – a short, squinty fellow —who looks at me, smirks and issues a single muffled guffaw, as if to say: even my relatively small cop penis is larger than this jerkoff's penis. If he only knew.

"Jack," says the detective, looking at me like I'm lunch and he's starving, "we need to talk about Friday."

Mon Aug 11 23:45:01 PDT 2008:

We talk in the Footwear History Library. Famous shoes, and digitally-antiqued photographs of the track-and-field stars who wore them to fame, shingle the walls. Shoved up against the famous footwear are commandeered desks and tables covered with hacked-together spare servers in crooked piles, some booted, some crashed, some with their guts spilling out their sides. A precarious tower of cannibalized workstation parts totters in one corner. The temperature is 81.5 degrees Fahrenheit. The whine of hard disks and cooling fans sounds like a swarm of killer bees. Color-coded data cable dangles from the ceiling, plugging into this and that. The Detective and I sit, facing, in ergonomic task chairs. The cops stand.

The Detective hands me a photograph. "You know this guy?"

The guy in the photo looks like your basic mullet-headed surf-Nazi.

"Dates a friend of yours? Drives a black Camaro?"

"I think I've seen him, yeah. Once or twice."

"Thrown a beer at him, ever?"

"*Once.*"

"Well, that's it. Once is all you get. Nobody gets to throw anything at Rock Short any more." The Detective snatches the photograph away.

"What do you mean ... is he dead?"

"*Oh,* yes. *Really* dead." The Detective places quotes around the word with his fingers. "'Dead', is the nice way to put it. 'Murdered,' is more correct, but still too nice. 'Brutally strangled and bludgeoned to death' is still actually leaving out the really nasty part of what happened to Rock Short. On Friday."

He leans close to me, leering at me with a consumed, fascinated expression, like I'm his pornography, like I'm turning him on. My head pounds ... I feel dizzy ... Lassie nudges me, taps on my knee. (Shut up, Lassie!)

"Wow," I reply. "Wow. That's really awful. Did you catch the guy?"

The Detective leaps up out of his chair and kicks it against the wall.

"Jack! Listen! I have a theory that you are really smart, okay! Maybe even smarter than me! So don't ask me stupid questions! You're connected, aren't you? In that room of yours? You've still got Internet. You know what's going on as well as anybody! It's the RFEs!"

RFEs?

My mind launches a desperate bubble-sort of its three-letter-acronym cache as Lassie starts to twitch and twist. RFEs? I read lots of RFCs, used to play an RME, correspond with EFR, I'm over-exposed to RF ... I look at the two officers and even they, behind their stoic cop facades, betray just a hint of WTF? regarding RFEs.

"The ... requests for enhancement?" I weakly suggest, my right foot tapping the floor.

Detective Dean glares meaningfully at his two cops, and they leave the room, shutting and locking it behind them.

"The RFEs. The Rampaging Fuckers of Everything. You know."

With all the facts hanging in the stale hot air of this room that I'd like to not know, I am really actually excited and happy to truly, utterly not know anything at all about this one.

"RFEs. Sorry ... please, tell me. RFEs?"

"You're an Internet guy. It's an Internet thing. That's how they organize! They're trading pictures in their chat-rooms and one-upping each other. Rampaging and fucking. Raping and killing. Do you have any idea how many people have been rampaged and fucked in this country in the last week? Men and women and *children*? And *pets*? Any idea? Venture a guess?"

"I've heard some stuff, but ... rumors!"

"I've *seen* some stuff. Photos! Yeah: because I am Homicide, because I hate murder and love peace and justice, I am the lucky fucker who gets to look at, and analyze, and organize and file that particular sickening, sick *cabinet* of photos! They thought it was one guy, and then they thought it was a gang of guys, but no, it's bigger. It's a *trend!* And I'm the cop, I'm the one who has to ... has to ... *aaaah!*"

For a moment I think he's going to hit me, or cry, or throw up. He pulls his hair and squeezes his face ... but then, robot-like, he switches it all off.

"Sorry, Jack. Rough couple of days. But hey: don't just take my word for it. Wanna see some photos, Jack? Hmm?"

Lassie ... heel!

He smiles, leering. "What is it, Jack? Can't sit still? Excited? You like the photos, right? How about DVDs, Jack? You like porno, don't you? C'mon, everybody likes porno. Snuff films? The hard stuff!"

"No! Excuse me, Detective, but you're grossing me out!"

Detective Dean throws back his head and laughs ... while, at what might be the least erotic moment of my entire life, Lassie strains against his seven plastic leashes. Bad Lassie! Down, boy!

Smiling Detective Dean: "Hey, okay, fine. Sorry. Forget about that, forget that. What about, you know ... what-do-they-call-em? Plastic toys. Of superheroes and stuff? Little rubber guys who fight and smash each other?"

"Collectable figurines."

"Fig-u-rines! Right! You collect 'em, don't you?"

"What's that got to do with anything? Yes!"

Lassie! Stop! That feels good, but ... stop!

"Where do you keep 'em?"

"At *home! Stop!*"

"Oh yeah? Where's home, Jack? Where do you live? 'Cause your boss doesn't know, and nobody else around here knows, and *I* sure don't know but, if I ask you where you were on Friday night and you say 'home' then, I'm like, I wanna know – Woah! Hey, you going somewhere?"

"No! My foot's asleep! *Sit!*" Detective Dean takes several steps back as I start stamping my foot on the floor. Oh, it twitches! It itches! It burns! Lassie!

"No. *I'll* stand. *You* sit."

Oh boy. "Listen, please ... Detective ... I haven't done anything, and I don't want to talk to you, and right now is a really shitty time anyway, and, just, I think you better leave."

"No. *I'll* stay. And *you'll* tell me whose blood we found

on your bean-bag!"

I flop down in the chair, and hear the muffled pop of a zip tie snapping near my knee. Blood roars in my ears. I'm getting light-headed. Staring at the ceiling. Oh no.

"Please, Detective —"

"Please, *shut up!* And then, after the blood issue, and the issue of your beef with Rock Short, we'll talk about the RFEs— because I really think a computer guy, an Internet guy like you, is who I need to talk to about that."

Oh, oh, oh. Oh no. Another zip tie pops. I lean back in my chair, closing my eyes. The feeling, the pain, the pressure is exquisite. Yellow dots squirm at the edges of my vision. The whine of disk drives and overworked air conditioning drills my ears while Lassie, oh, Lassie ... you scoundrel, Lassie!

The Detective looms over me, sneering. I am pale and weak and tingly all over.

"But then, Jack, what I really want to know is: who else? I know you didn't do it alone. That I cannot picture. Those two badges in the hall can't picture it either, and they've seen all *kinds* of guys kill all *kinds* of guys. But you? Against Rock Short? You against *anybody*? Hah! Don't think so!"

Pop! Pop! Oh fuck. Oh no. Oh Lassie, please don't do that! Please don't make me want you to do that!

"How did you do it?" he demands. "Who helped you? What did you *use?*" Then he hears the snapping sound, looks down ... inspects my twitching pant leg, and the angry hostage struggling beneath. His eyes quiver with curiosity.

"Whatcha packing there, Jack?" Staring right into my eyes he reaches a slow hand toward the top pocket on the right thigh of my parachute pants BUT

Despite all this, despite the terrible truths in this room, despite the proximity of the sweat-stinking Detective's hand, electrical messages of pure happiness and romantic affection and wholesome copulation begin to gather in my fingers and toes, the back of my neck, the tip of my tongue, tickling my nipples and my anus, my knees, my hips, my spine, rushing, throbbing, pounding, pushing through me, jerking me around AND

Detective Dean freezes and stares, with utter stupid confusion mixed with revulsion and a hint of concern, at the shape in my pocket WHEN

Tue Aug 12 00:00:00 PDT 2008:

Like a whip, like a bear-trap, like a cobra striking, large, long, thick and terrifying: Lassie the Monster Cock bursts through my pant leg with a noisy slash, seizes Detective Dean by the neck and throttles him with stiff, white turgid clenches ... of PLEASURE!

But Lassie ... wait ... no! Slow down, Lassie! This is wrong ... I'm not into this! Please, let's try something else ... I try to pull him off but I can't even reach around him with both hands now. Oh Jesus, Lassie ... you're bigger than the both of us!

The Detective scuffles weakly at the floor with his treadless cop shoes, he claws desperately at your veiny flesh around his neck, Lassie, as you hoist him higher. You push, and you squeeze, and with your remaining length you smack and smash and batter the fat purple hammer of your head against his red, puffed up face, stabbing and bludgeoning over and over, demanding entrance to his ears, his nose, his eyes.

Lassie, stop! I am not comfortable with this! I don't like it, Lassie!

We fall to the floor, a tangle of desperate limbs struggling in a puddle of blood and teeth. I jam my feet against the Detective's chest and head and pull with all the strength in my legs, as my testes start to quiver. Don't make me do this, Lassie! Don't make me feel like this while you do that!

A single muffled gurgle of defiance escapes the Detective's throat. He pounds uselessly with his fists. I want to call for help but I'm hyperventilating, quaking, out of breath ...

Cable management! I reach my pocket and find one extra-large zip tie—a size I always carry but never seem to need. I wrap it around the root, the base, the interlink ... and I pull it tight with both of my weak hands. And you'd better believe: it hurts!

Bad Lassie! Bad penis! Not Allowed! Down! Straight to bed you go! I am cinching the strap, yanking upward as the wire-reinforced plastic zip-tie digs deep into our flesh!

The pain jabs through us like a rusty razor. You whip around to see, your three little white eyes full of dumb animal murder. With your remaining length you swat at me, but you can't quite reach all the way from my crotch to his neck, around that twice and all the way back to my face, not yet, not quite ... so you wrap yourself once more around the policeman's head. You're mad, Lassie, you are just furious, oh yes, you are thrashing, squeezing, raging, hissing and spitting! I've got the tip of the zip-tie between my teeth, I'm pulling with all my back and shoulders as I'm pushing with all my legs as you are throbbing, clenching, tightening, as Detective Dean struggles, weakly ...

I feel like I'm ripping out my own insides ... and I think we're going to come.

Detective Dean shudders and out a last gagging puff of air, and Lassie dives deep down the dead policeman's throat! Cramming deeper as the wave begins to crest, as I being to scream! The pain! The flesh! The body and the blood! The blood!

With a ripping, a snapping, and a wet, foetal POP ... Lassie drops our connection, unplugs, slips her leash. A massive weight and leverage falls away from me, a deep ache replaces it, and I'm alone.

Lassie slinks under a corner table with his meal, trailing the tips of vessels we once shared. I observe him keenly, watching him feed: he regurgitates a steaming pink venom, pumping it into the dead man's head and down his throat. Then: crawling deeper, squeezing earthwormlike down the bulging dead neck, exploring the entrails, sniffing and tasting. Exiting from his ass or some self-torn opening a few minutes later, and finally peeping, slick with gore and shit, from a pant leg. A small silver tongue or proboscis flits in and out of Lassie's tiny mouth, licking the blood away from his three little eyes that stare at me, innocently, questioningly.

"Oh, Lassie! You bad, bad penis! How could you?"
Lassie cowers in the dead policeman's pant leg, shy, afraid. Ashamed.
"Lassie! You can't kill policemen! You can't eat people! You're for sex, Lassie! For human pleasure!"
Lassie slithers out of the pant legs, head hung low, whimpering like a pup. Lassie is sorry.
"Look, I know you were trying to protect me. Probably. Right?"
Lassie sits up, staring at me. Blood on his chin. His ragged tail wagging. And those eyes ... my penis ... my big little Lassie ...
"Lassie ... you killed Rock too, didn't you? The surf-Nazi?"
Lassie bobs up and down, proud, excited, happy.
"Oh Lassie ... what will I do with you?"

That really excellent and pressing question—what to do, exactly, with my seven-foot-long bloodthirsty pet anaconda cock-monster, who just ripped free of my crotch and ate the policeman who thinks I murdered the abusive boyfriend of Angela Fine— and another, perhaps even more pressing question—how do I explain all this to Angela Fine, and make her understand that I did it all for her, for love, and how beautiful that is, and that the evil, morally repugnant part I didn't even do myself, not exactly, because I am so good, but at least she is now free, safe, Rock can't crush her any more, and that I love her more than love itself and will take care of her forever and make her happy in every way that doesn't specifically require me having a penis any more – these two questions overwrite each other, back and forth, on the filesystem of my head, consuming me, hanging me, crashing me ...

Because I am desperate to feel less weird, I grab a roll of duct tape from the parts pile and tape shut the crotch of my shredded parachute pants. As I do so I glimpse the empty socket, the disconnected port of flesh, the land where proud, mighty genitals once roamed ... oh god ...

And then I see nothing at all, because power, finally, fails. The deafening whir of tiny high-speed spinning things spins down, slowly, to silence and a phantom ringing in my ears. The failure has finally reached us.

On the other side of the Footwear History Library door I hear an approaching scuttle of footsteps, and then an urgent pounding at the door and jingling of keys. Above me I hear a rattling of dangling data cable and a knocking aside of ceiling panels. I try to find my voice ...

"Who is it?"

It's the Chad Squad. "Jack? Are you done in there? We seriously need you in Trouble."

Tue Aug 12 00:17:40 PDT 2008:

Good morning! It's a brand new day, and already the Trouble Center is teetering on the edge of the following gaping chasm of Trouble: the spam has sidestepped our Maginot Line, jumping the firewall in Shenzhou instead, and is pouring in through the VPN, choking us; ours is the last stable electrical grid in America; Rampaging Fuckers of Everything are apparently less rumored and more actual than initially estimated—rampaging and fucking nationwide, trans-continentally, and even in Europe, according to Netops Grunt Two, who has cleverly jury-rigged an API satellite news feed to a small barricaded zone under his desk, where he has hoarded supplies, and which he refuses to leave. The Army and the National Guard and the INS are incommunicado, missing, presumed fucked. The Air Force is in midair and intends to stay there. The President is underground. Homeland Security has fled.

Also: Phil Tong has a gun, he has Gregg Lotz in a half-nelson, and he wants us to "stop the Internet"—not just our small fragment of Internet but the whole world-wide shebang—for reasons that he can't articulate. Grunt One asked him to file a ticket, and is now bleeding from a hole in his neck.

And me? I cannot deal. I cannot deal at all! Impossible hell is tumbling down on me from all sides! Chad W. and Chad D. look at me with infinite reserves of tiredness in their eyes, waiting for me to finish crying.

I want my figurines! I want Angela! If I found her, if we ran away together, would it matter? Have the RFEs already gotten her? What can we do, Chad and Chad and Gregg and I, about trouble on this level? Does anything in Trouble Center matter, really, compared to the last half-hour?

Blood drips down my pant leg. "Guys, I'm injured. I need ..."

Chad and Chad, short guys both, look up at me out of the depths of their ongoing shock, wincing for the next impact. Chad Wankel's twitchy eye twitches, and Chad Day rubs his moustache. How could I ever explain? How much Trouble can we take? We are such a shambles, our department of IT professionals. Such a ridiculous cast of misfits we are, in all ways but one.

I don't know what else to do, I really don't. Chad and Chad wait, needing to act, needing to fix, needing to support the IT mission. It is our purpose. It is all we know.

So I send them to yank all the WADSLAPs, take us off-line ... and then I enter the Trouble Center, cockless, alone.

Tue Aug 12 00:23:11 PDT 2008:
Something's wrong with Phil Tong. He's sitting upon Gregg Lotz, on the institutional gray carpet floor in the center of the Trouble Center. Under the sodium vapor emergency backup lights his skin is blue and corpse-like. His breathing is shallow. Something is causing him pain—he's curled up in a ball, clutching his belly, pointing his gun at Gregg, then at me. Gregg, a portrait of stillness and fear, still manages in a single glance to communicate all of mid-upper-management's anxieties.

"Shut it down!" roars Phil. "Cut it off! It's got to die!"

I scavenge, deep through my soul, for a kind, understanding tone of voice to use with Phil Tong.

"Phil, listen," I finally say, "Please ... there's things we can do, and things we can't."

"Don't tell me you don't know, Jack! Hah! I've been watching you."

"What have you been watching me do, Phil? Tighten the D-Links?"

Phil is momentarily confused. "No ... the treatment!" he says, leveling a finger at me. "The cure."

His eyes quiver with madness and pain. He's not, he must, he's ...

"It's hellfire! The devil's on the network! Jack ... he's uploaded me! And he's uploaded you! And he's coming out! He's coming out! Oh yes! The Internet is a vein of contagion!"

"I ... I don't disagree with you, Phil, but the verb 'to upload' —"

"Good and evil, Jack! Not ones and zeroes. *Evil!*"

"Listen, Phil, the Internet is literally millions of miles of fiber-optics and copper cable —"

"Maggots! Worms! Demons!"

"—millions of routers in millions of places, around the world, we *can't* just switch it on and off for you like a desk lamp! It's a system, with procedures! And administrators, IT professionals—"

He snorts in utter, utter contempt.

"—are working night and day right now to *solve* this! Things are going to get better, Phil! This is all going to pass ... in a few days ..."

Phil Tong gives me a you're-such-an-idiot expression so heartfelt it's almost touching. He looks at the back of Gregg Lotz's whimpering head, looks at his gun ... and kneels on Gregg's back in humble prayer, whispering the words under his hitching, shallow breath. He's blue as a vein. Bleeding.

"Okay Phil: the cure, yes. Bad. Very bad. I know that now! *I'm not stupid.*"

He's gotten to thy will be done ...

"But I don't see what that's got to do with the network!"

... he's on the daily bread ... the trespasses ...

"What do you know that I don't know, Phil? Phil?"

.. received the delivery ... entered the kingdom ...

"Phil, tell me what you know! Phil!"

... the power, the glory, forever ... Amen.

And the brains of Phil Tong rain down on us like tickets.

Tue Aug 12 00:29:23 PDT 2008
I stagger out the back door of Trouble as cops and guards and mid-upper-management pour in the front. No more Trouble, please. I'm done. I just want some diet Fresca.

I stumble through the emergency-lit hallways to the drink-snack-shuffleboard court, but the Fresca machine is down, so I run off towards the wiring closet to grab a spare fifty foot power cord so I can bring up the Fresca machine on redundant power, because that, I know, will work, and I need to fix something very badly right now. Passing a window I look out on the International Sportswear Campus and see a field of red and white and blue spinning lights. A rising tide of cops is licking the shoreline of International Sportswear. Searching for their fallen brother.

And I hear things in the ceiling. Oh God I do.

I grab the cord and a few more cable ties. I take the long way back, through Information Receiving, through Marketing-Weightlifting, down the stairs, past the conference gym, up the stairs, past the padded offices of mid-upper management, around through Payroll and back to the drink-snack-shuffleboard court, and I listen:

Things are definitely in the ceiling. Big things.

I run down the hall to the nearest wiring closet and find some redundant power in the very last redundant power jack, and run it back and climb under the Fresca machine to find a sticky, sugary mess and a total, utter failure of cable management. The minimum-wage soda techs who drive around servicing these machines are always watching the clock and just don't give a damn. I unknot and untwist and unplug all the cords from the one sticky power strip and try each of them, one at a time, in my live cable, until I see the backlit plastic close-up of the Fresca bubbles blink to life.

I fill my cup with ice and diet Fresca, and sip it, listening to the ceiling things.

Everybody has a drug. Mine is diet Fresca. And porn, too, I suppose ... but mostly diet Fresca. It keeps me steady, helps me think. It's all I have at this sad, mad moment. I am detail oriented. The whole forest is crackling with hellfire, but if I can focus on this tree I might survive.

The ceiling things are restless. They're coming and going, wandering around, exploring. Searching.

Downstairs, expensive panes of corporate glass shatter dramatically. Cop radios cackle with nervous cop talk. I really don't think this is a good time for me to talk to them. I need to disappear.

Tue Aug 12 00:41:28 PDT 2008

On my way to the Offline Backup Storage Vault, I run straight into Angela Fine!

Who sees me, and screams.

"Angela! Hey! Shhh!" Angela is panting, staring, a terrified, trapped thing. She's wearing a bathrobe and an oversized men's leather jacket, the sort of thing Rock would wear. She's clutching it tightly around her and stroking the leather lapel with the long, slender fingers of one hand. Her hair is all messy but it smells like summer, and there is nobody I could ever be more happy to see. I grab her and hold her and show her I'm friendly.

Downstairs and far away, the police announce through megaphones: WE ARE THE POLICE!

"Jack ..." Angela stands perfectly stock still, rigid and trembling, with a painful, worried smile on her beautiful round face. I step back.

"Angela ... wow! Hi! It's ... funny you're here!"

Her beautiful brown eyes stare unblinking into mine.

"Jack ... what's that on you?"

"Oh, gee ... brains I think. Phil Tong's. Sorry."

She whimpers, and stares.

Downstairs and far away, the police blare: COME OUT NOW!

"Angela ... can I get you a Fresca?"

Her voice is a quiet, desperate squeak. "Please don't kill me, Jack."

Oh no. This is completely backwards.

"Angela ... no! No way, never *ever* would I do that!"

"Okay! Sorry!" She's frozen like a deer in the headlights.

"No, *really* you have to believe me! I didn't kill that guy. Your boyfriend? Whoever. It wasn't me!"

"Okay. I believe you. Just ... don't kill me" she sobs, terrified and sad.

"I've been worried, actually, about you! With all this stuff happening ... Angela, what are you even *doing* here?"

Downstairs and far away, the police yell: WE ARE COMING IN!

"They brought me here," she says, nodding toward the loud stairwell, "they want me to talk to you. Actually ..." She breathes in a deep breath of air, shakes her beautiful head, exhales sweet perfume. "I don't really know why they brought me. I don't think they know what they're doing. They're just running all over, acting like cops. They're scared. They're losing. They say you raped all those people, and ..."

Downstairs and far away, the police yell: THIS IS YOUR LAST CHANCE!

"Angela, please please please don't be afraid of me. I'm a really, really nice guy. I *don't* rape people. I don't even hit people! I'm not big, and I'm not muscular, and I don't have a big ... I don't have a big Camaro, but ... but I'm nice! And I'm gentle! And I'm incredibly sensitive, and a keen observer! And I like you. I've always liked you."

"I like you too, Jack ... please don't kill me."

This is totally wrong, so sad and wrong and awful ... "Angela! *Hello?* Are you hearing any of this? Don't be afraid!

Look, I wanted to show you ... I've been ... Oh, Angela ..."
    Police: IF YOU DON'T COME OUT, WE'RE COMING IN! THIS IS YOUR LAST AND FINAL CHANCE!
    "Angela, I've got something really important to tell you!"
    "Sure Jack! Whatever you say, just ..."

If Angela had said "just please don't kill me," I would have continued to not kill her, and to instead reassure her, and be nice to her, and maybe eventually she would have begun to believe me. And then maybe we could have moved from that topic to other, related topics: things we both like, stuff we could go do together sometime, if things were ever normal again. Or we could have just kept on talking, which would be enough for all eternity, just to talk with Angela Fine.
    If Angela had said "just hold me," I would have held her tightly in my arms forever with all my strength, enveloping her in everything good that I am, and maybe she would have felt the warmth of my heart and the pure love radiating from it, and believed me.
    If Angela had said "just come downstairs and talk to the policemen," I would have done that for her, sure, and who knows what might have happened next, with the world crashing, dumping core, going up in rampaging, fucking smoke all around us, but at least she would have seen that I was trying, and maybe, eventually, she would have had an opportunity to look into my heart, and believe me.
    But if Angela had said "just please don't let a twenty-foot long monster cock suddenly reach down from the ceiling and scoop me up in its sick bulging skin and yank me screaming into the crawlspace ..."
    Then I would have had to disappoint her.
    Because it got me too.

```
date: command not found
```

It's dark, I can't breathe, I am dragged, scraped, crushed, sliced, raked through metal and wire and fiberglass and dust and heat and cold and darkness. I pass out, I wake up, I scream, I pass out again ...

I come to on a floor somewhere, a floor with scorching hot under-floor forced air blowing in my face, to crackling static and deep, angry pounding. Tongues of flame rise from the corners of the room. Smoke obscures the ceiling. Some living, writhing thing is climbing all over me! Snakes! The floor is carpeted with snakes! I scramble to my knees, but I mustn't stand up, it's a fire! A fire in Ice Station Zebra. With snakes. But where is Angela?

I hear her gasping, weeping ... I see her.

She's held face-down on the floor by writhing, squirming cables! Power cables, data cables, fiber, copper, wriggling together in a seething mass, binding her, crawling over her, plucking at her robe and jacket. Tongues of uncoiled backup tape unwind from the gaping maw of the tape backup jukebox and lick between her legs. She screams.

Beside her, in the center of the room, rises a thick, undulating tower of meat where WADSLAP Interchange 01 is supposed to be. Or rather: coiled tightly around the rack formerly known as WADSLAP Interchange 01 is an unspeakably large, long, thick and terrifying three-eyed devil penis, slamming its head against the top of the rack, over and over. My penis. My little monster.

"Lassie! What are you doing!?"

58

The pounding stops. The monster cock stretches toward me, nudges me playfully with a scarred, black-blue head, a head larger than my own ... it licks my cheek with its long, silver tongue and stares at me with its sad white eyes.

"Lassie ... what are you *doing?*"

Lassie unwinds himself from WADSLAP Interchange 01, and the snakes on the floor clear a path for me. I step towards the rack to inspect its status.

On the front side of the rack, I see that Chad and Chad did everything I asked them: they pulled the data, the power, the flash cards and the hot-swappable drives from every WADSLAP, severing all our Internet links four different ways. The demon cables stab and poke, jacking and unjacking the open ports of the dead units, but the non-volatile boot media is nowhere evident. These links will stay down.

On the back side of the rack, I see ... Chad and Chad!

Their bodies are crushed and squeezed into a barely-recognizable blue-black pulp of limb, hair, blood and company t-shirt, jammed into the nine-inch slot between the WADSLAPs and the power conditioner. Crumpled, swollen, bloody-nailed fingers jut out in all directions.

I can't deal. Oh god.

Lassie taps me on the shoulder, and then ... he rubs the side of his head softly against Angela's thigh, as she screams and struggles, and the cables grip her tighter.

"What's that, Lassie? You mean ... you want me to reconnect the Internet ... and then we'll rape Angela Fine together?"

Lassie nods and wags his massive testicles enthusiastically, slapping them hard against the side of another nearby rack, knocking it sideways, shaking down charred panels from the ceiling.

I did this! I did it with my new penis. Oh God. It's me, it's my own flesh, my own cancer!

"Lassie ... oh God, Lassie ... why can't you be a good penis?"

59

Lassie nods and wags, wags and nods. The cables on the floor are watching us curiously.

"You're not a bad penis, are you?"

Lassie shakes his head, vehemently: no!

"Lassie, listen to me: raping and killing ... that's not nice. Those are bad things."

Lassie's tail stops wagging.

"Lassie, you're a good penis, but you've got to stop this. Stop killing, Lassie!"

Lassie shakes his head, no. All of the snakes on the floor shake their heads, no.

"Lassie?"

Lassie shoves me up against the WADSLAP rack and bangs furiously against the side.

"No, Lassie! I won't do it. It's wrong."

Lassie stares at me with his three sad eyes ... and then cudgels me in the ribs. I spit Fresca and tumble across the floor.

The serpent rises above me like a fist, as blue and pink Cat 5 cables seize my wrists and ankles, strapping them down! Pink saliva burbles from the monster's head and drips down on my shin, sizzling, smoking, burning.

The giant penis coils back to strike ....

And then the charred, smoldering giant penis of Phil Tong falls out of the ceiling on top of it.

The two monster penises wrestle and strike and bite and punch one another, knocking over the telco rack and the backup tower and the application server. Chairs and tables and bits of machines skitter and crash across the room. The snakes hiss and clutch and dart around. They release us to wrap around Phil Tong's unholy soot-smeared penis, which has not three eyes but four, and which is much, much, bigger than mine.

Angela and I crawl out the door the door as the two vast muscular coils of evil meat tumble and pound and mutilate each other, knocking apart the data center and, even now, growing larger ...

We scramble on our hands and knees past Payroll, the smoke just a foot above us, as the building shakes and windows shatter. We tumble down the stairs and scramble across the broken glass of the Hall of Sports Heroes as deep, serpentine screeching fills the air.

We run out onto the lawn. The rampaged bodies of fucked policemen litter the landscape.

Something explodes. We keep running, towards the empty cop cars in the Field Of Dreams And Parking. Shrapnel of office equipment smashes down like comets. A spinning executive desk falls through the sky and shatters into sawdust on the ground in front of us. Angela is nearly crushed by a photocopier. A flaming shoe—worn by Jesse Owens during his heroic sweep of the track and field events at the 1939 Berlin Olympics—smacks me in the head. We keep running.

The nearest squad car is still idling with its doors open. I don't actually have a driver's license, but I'm very good with machines. We slam the doors and start moving, oh so slowly, out onto Campus and toward Victory, to the interstate, west, to the coast. To the ocean. Somewhere, there must be somewhere we can go. At least we're together now: Angela, curled up in a weeping ball in the back seat, and me, the New Me ... what's left of him.

In my rear view mirror I see them still: the two bloody monsters, larger than buildings, longer than highways, thicker than mountains, rolling and crushing and fighting and biting, rampaging and fucking over the entire earth.

Sun Jan 01 06:06:06 XST 2013

There really was a time before the worms. I remember.

Back in that time, almost everybody lived on land. And there were millions of people, back then. Billions of us.

And land was beautiful, and full of life. Before the worms came.

People ate all kinds of foods, and did all kinds of things, and had everything, on land.

But now there is only the sea, and the worms with their teeth, and the giant brutal holes they bore into the earth, and the ooze that pours out. And us, just the last precious few of us, the boat people, hanging on out here on the stinking brown sea. Scraping out a living on the shitting planet of the ramping fuckers of everything.

We hunt the worms, we eat the worms ... and the worms hunt and eat us.

Call me Ishmael.

JOURNEY TO THE CENTER OF AGNES CUDDLEBOTTOM

For Sam Henderson

Q: How did it feel, being the first man ever to set foot inside the rectum of Agnes Cuddlebottom?

DR. EMIL MULLER-FOKKER, M.D., C.R.S., G.I.D.:

The lining of the distal rectum felt rough and leathery, and slightly clammy. Venous protrusions and the slickness of the mucous made for rough going in the region just beyond the internal anal sphincter, but with the special climbing gear we designed for the operation, I was soon able to reach an area of greater traction and establish a base camp just beyond the inferior rectal valve. In that area the mucosa had a slight gravelly texture, similar to a badly potholed parking lot, due to fistulae and an unusual accretion of crystallized urea.

Q: I mean, historically. Did you, Doctor Fokker, recognize the historic import?

A: Yes, of course, the historic import was obvious to all. Certainly nobody had ever done this before, although in theory the possibility had existed for some time. But as a physician, my first responsibility was to Mrs. Cuddlebottom, and my main concern, throughout the operation, was to find and remove the obstruction that was killing her, and to return her to her full health.

Q: To the degree that an 80-year-old heroin addict can be said to recover full health.

A: Well, some peoples' health is fuller than other peoples' health. It's true that Mrs. Cuddlebottom's overall condition was deeply degenerate. The patina of a long and traumatic life colored every part of her, especially her rectal cavity. The normally supple rectal folds were dry and crusty like a sun-baked desert floor, and a cloudy, foul-smelling excretion oozed from the cracks between the anal columns.

Q: You don't say.

A: In fact, it was the inadvisability of the surgical approaches to acute exacerbations of chronic upper intestinal constipation, and the failure of standard drug therapies, plus her lapse into coma, that activated the clause of her patient consent form which made her a candidate for this, as you say, historic procedure.

Q: Weren't you afraid? How did you know you wouldn't be killed by this crazy Spinejack device?

A: I had reservations, initially. The procedure seemed dangerous, if not impossible. But the science behind the principle was sound, the funding was lined up, and Doctor Spinejack convinced me it could be done. So we had a team of graduate students build the apparatus, and assist us in intensive testing. In order to assure the safety of the Spinejack Transform, my colleague Doctor Spinejack and our team at Mount Venuda University Hospital first sent a small houseplant through the machine, and then a laboratory test subject.

Q: You mean Jojo the Chimp?

A: Yes. Using wireless transmitters, we were able to monitor Jojo's health and knew he made it through okay. That's what convinced the entire medical team that we could do this, could treat Mrs. Cuddlebottom from the inside, and in doing so, make history.

Q: But the tragic events that unfolded thereafter ... did you foresee those?

A: What?

Q: Did you foresee the unfolding of the tragic events?

A: Of course not! Look, don't try to pin that on me, I am a physician and I did what I thought was urgently necessary to improve the condition of a dying patient.

Q: Right. How could you have foreseen the tragic events?

A: How could anyone? We live in difficult times. Tragic events are commonplace. The non-localized conflict, the economic unwinding, the environmental collapse ... things are tough all over. But I'm a gastroenterologist, and my job is to heal the sick. Agnes Cuddlebottom came to our clinic in a great deal of pain.

Q: Uninsured, no doubt.

A: That's not my concern! Certainly there are wealthier, healthier recta we could have used to test the Spinejack Transform. But this rectum needed us. How could we refuse?

Q: Doctor Spinejack, how does your Spinejack Transform actually work?

DR. OTTO SPINEJACK, PH.D., PHYSICIST:

Well. Our device harnesses newly discovered principles from the field of string theory and hyper-spatial symmetric analysis, in order to create an N-dimensional Impedance Transform Intersection. The theory of this we first published, myself and my colleagues Ed Ruff and Louise Vanhoff, in our paper in the Journal of Relativistic Physics three years ago entitled: "*Implanting People In The Rectums Of Other People: Finally We Can!*"

Q: Can you explain it in layman's terms?

A: I will try. To understand the principles, it will help you to picture how a brass musical instrument, such as the tuba, takes a very tiny sound and amplifies it. It does this by allowing a pressure wave to expand very slowly within a long tubular chamber of increasing diameter, following precise exponential rules in a controlled fashion, until it emerges with a powerful "Ooom-pah" sound that you may know from the classics. Or, if you prefer, Polka.

Q: Okay, I'm picturing that ...

A: Our machine, of course, creates a tube of folded N-space instead of brass, by using quantum computation to remove the entropy from a powerful field of strong nuclear forces. And our machine blows this tuba in reverse, injecting large spacetime-waves in the large end, then folding them inward through higher dimensions, as they travel up through this tubing, growing smaller and smaller. Otherwise, it is exactly the same.

Q: So it's a sort of a reverse-polkafying device?

A: You could give it that name, yes. However, the process, while theoretically promising, is unstable in real-world situations, as the space-fabric, exiting the small end of this tube, would mismatch the surrounding space-time impedance so dramatically that explosive re-expansion would occur, and boom! You die.

Q: Then how are you able to—

A: The breakthrough, yes: we realized, mathematically, that if the transform intersection could be mated with a very specific shape and length and form of tubular chamber, the space-time impedance could in fact be matched, so the re-expansion effect is countered, and in fact the N-space folding continues as long as forward momentum is maintained. So easy, yes?

Q: If you say so, yes.

A: But no! The tubular chamber for this is so very specific. It must match the material being folded in various ways, it needs a certain length and shape, also temperature, and many other mathematical properties. It would be impossible to manufacture such a chamber ... yet, amazingly, it occurs in nature! It is as if a Creator invented this chamber for this very purpose! Because the human gastro-intestinal tract, you see, is actually a perfect match for the Spinejack transform! Human beings are the missing piece!

Q: So, your invention is not the general-purpose matter reducer that some have called it.

A: Yes and no. Yes, we can shrink anything you want. But no, it has to go in the anus.

TRANSCRIBED EXCERPT FROM THE VOICE RECORDER OF DR. FOKKER DURING HIS JOURNEY THROUGH THE CUDDLEBOTTOM RECTUM:

DF: 11:19am Thursday August 9th ... I'm standing on the soft floor of the patient's rectal lining, at the bottom of the sigmoid colon. The climb to here was nearly vertical, but now the surface is leveling out some. I'm removing my crampons, which induced hemorrhaging, and am switching to a pair of sturdy hiking boots.

There's an odor of intestinal gas here that's strong but not overwhelming. The sigmoid colon gapes before me, a vast cavern of mystery. The light from my headlamp barely penetrates the dark, looming blackness. Down over my shoulder I can still make out the internal anal sphincter, squinting up from the depths like some huge mad eye. It's awe-inspiring. I've dissected cadaver specimens of this area of the body in school, seen it on colonoscopic video, I know it in detail, but to actually stand here in this passageway and inhabit it as a natural landscape ... words fail me! It's beautiful! Truly, this is a new frontier.

I've just stepped in what appear to be feces! Fascinating! There's a thin, crumbly layer of it on the rectal floor, not enough to form a stool. There's so much to study here ... but I mustn't tarry. The patient's health is my first priority. This is just the first step in a long journey. Somewhere far, far down this amazing tunnel of life, the mysterious obstruction that is killing Agnes Cuddlebottom is hiding, waiting.

But first, I must find Jojo the chimp, our test subject. He's in here somewhere. I'm extracting a bag of goldfish crackers from my medical kit, and rattling it over my head. He loves these.

Jojo? Can you hear me? It's Emil! Where are you, Jojo?

Jojo! Here he comes, he recognizes me. I'm giving him a handful of goldfish ... he appears healthy. No apparent injury, no listlessness. He's got some fecal matter on his hands and feet, and his coat, but no other visible contusions or abrasions. We monitored his health from outside but it's good to see that he's a healthy, happy monkey. Great to see you, Jojo.

What's that? Jojo is communicating something to me, using the sign language system he learned in the behavioral heath lab. Say it again, Jojo.

JOJO AFRAID. JOJO WANT HOME.

Poor monkey. Of course this is all very confusing for him. Nevertheless, Jojo's crucial role in this operation will be as forward scout; his natural agility will serve us well, and if there are any fluctuations in the N-dimensional folding effect as we travel up the intestines, Jojo will experience them first.

Jojo is still signing: JOJO HOME HOME HOME. HATE POOP BAD POOP.

Obviously we would never place Jojo in any kind of jeopardy, intentionally. We are doctors, and he's a good monkey. But since the Spinejack Transform is so new, based as it is on the new physics, there's a certain risk of the unknown here that Jojo will help us to manage. By going first, ahead of me. Trailblazing. It's a historic role, for a very special animal. It's more than he understands, but his job in this procedure will enshrine him in the annals of medicine.

I sign to Jojo: BANANA TREE THAT WAY. And off he ambles up the slope. Good monkey!

Q: Is it true that you are the first reporter to set foot in the rectum of Agnes Cuddlebottom?

BRENDA SPONGE, WPMS CHANNEL 23 NEWS COMMENTATOR:
You're darn tootin'.

Q: Do you have any medical or scientific training?

A: I'm a broadcast journalist, I studied broadcast journalism at Columbia U. And I'm a woman.

Q: But how did you manage, finding yourself shrunken to microscopic size, and thrust into this other woman's—

A: All part of the job. I've done war zones, I've done burning buildings, I do a lot of tsunamis. I'm where the story is. And this place, this rectum of this old lady, with globby things all over the ceiling and shit everywhere ... it was crazy disgusting, yeah, but no tsunami. I'm used to being shot at, you know? Bombs falling, bloody dead people everyplace. As soon as I got my leg free of that big nasty squeezy fucker—

Q: The internal anal sphincter.

A: —yeah, hated that! Oh boy! But then when I stood up on my two feet, I knew I could tough this out. So with my videographer Sam on that fiberoptic ass camera thing I filed my first report from Base Camp right then and there.

Q: What was the crux of your story?

A: It's on video, you can watch it yourself. Here, I've got it on my phone. I was moving so fast I didn't even check wardrobe. Look, you can see Cuddlebottom-shit on my lapel.

Q: But what was your intention, jumping into this delicate medical situation? What story were you chasing?

A: Human interest. Life and death, the technology beat, all that. The story of a woman on the brink of death and the amazing new technology that could save her life! Of course I had to fight to get it shown, as usual. Dino, my station head, didn't want to touch it. Issues of taste, he said. Really it's because I'm a woman, and to Dino this was just a women's health issue, and that's not news to Dino. He had a boy-in-a-well story he was hot to lead with that night. But whaddya know: it dried up. Turns out the boy's not a boy, he's an old hobo, and then he dies, and everybody's like, so what? Suddenly Dino has to fill time, so my segment led at nine o'clock because it had to. And from there the story took off like an Airbus.

Q: Your first report was picked up by over 300 affiliates nationwide.

A: That's right. And the second, and the third. Which proves, among other things, that women's health issues really do make gripping, touching news stories, stories that can compete with the wars and the famines and all the gritty, down-tempo stuff. Not to toot my own horn here, but I'm proud that WPMS was able to bring the problems of women like Agnes Cuddlebottom into the public consciousness. That lady has suffered, let me tell you. Did you know she was a prostitute?

Q: How long did your scoop of the Cuddlebottom rectum last?

A: Oh, the other local affiliates were in the hospital within minutes. Pretty soon we had three or four of those fiber optic ass camera things bumping around like flashlights on a snake, looking for a fresh angle. But no reporters had the guts yet, to get embedded like I did. So I got the first interview with the good doctor, which was smooth as silk. Emil's a natural: very articulate, great cheekbones, knows when to shut up. I followed him all the way up to the sigmoid colon, dangling from a rope, reporting live as it happened. Then at the top I met Jojo, we did Jojo's Story, and that absolutely *killed*. We raked in the Nielsens.

Q: That was a beautiful segment.

A: Thank you. What can I say? People love monkeys. But it takes guts and sensitivity to bring home that kind of story.

Q: Tell me, what was the nature of your financial arrangement with Doctor Spinejack?

A: The what of my what with who?

Q: Didn't your station pay Doctor Spinejack a sum, in exchange for exclusive news access to Agnes Cuddlebottom's rectum?

A: I don't have to answer that.

Q: We're just trying to piece together the events.

A: No comment.

Q: How they unfolded, and became tragic.

A: Yeah, you and me both. Anyway, that was only for the first twenty-four hours, just to give us a leg up. After that, it's a free country. And after twenty-four hours, boy did the circus come to town.

Q: Are you the members of Agnes Cuddlebottom's medical team, excepting Doctor Spinejack?

THE MEMBERS OF DR. FOKKER'S MEDICAL TEAM, EXCEPTING DR. SPINEJACK:
Yup. That's us.

Q: How did you manage the sudden media attention around your patient, Agnes Cuddlebottom?

A: It sucked, deeply. Although our patient was hooked to life support systems and a nutrient drip, her vitals remained delicate, and there was a constant threat of complications due to the respirators, the IVs, and of course the Spinejack Device attached to her anus. Our nerves were on edge, as we followed Doctor Fokker and Jojo's ascent through unknown, potentially dangerous conditions, towards the mysterious obstruction. It was exciting, but draining.

Q: I see.

A: But then, as Mrs. Cuddlebottom's treatment became a national media event, it got ridiculous! On top of our other difficulties, now we had this invasion of media people, constantly demanding interviews, access, coffee and pastries, directions to the bathroom, power outlets for their phones and laptops. Maintaining a sterile environment became impossible. The installation of more and more colonoscopic equipment took up valuable space in the operating theater, and we went through

K-Y Jelly like it was ketchup at a hot dog stand. Why every network felt they needed their own coloscopist, we will never get. Some union thing, they said. Our nurses had to elbow past cameramen, gaffers and best boys just to change the patient's drip. Plus, during all this, the funds issue grew more and more acute.

Q: Funds issue? What funds?

A: Right, there weren't any funds, that was the issue. After Doctor Spinejack's grant money ran out, we were no longer officially on the case. Due to the patient's egregious lack of insurance—she entered the hospital under false pretenses, claiming to be an heir to the James Brown fortune—Facilities Management, the bottom-line people, disapproved of expenditures toward her care, even though the Spinejack Device could clearly usher in a lucrative new field of therapy. But we believed in what we were doing, we believed in Doctor Spinejack and didn't want to let him down.

Q: How did you manage?

A: We all worked double shifts, donating our time. First we would care for all the other patients on our normal rotations, then we'd sneak into Obstetrics to sneak extra tubes of KY into the deep pockets of our lab coats, and then head back to look after Agnes. Sleep came in short bursts between crises. It was like first year rotations all over again, and did any of us miss that? No sir.

Q: Sleeping in closets, under tables ...

A: Napping on cots in the operating theater, in the cafeteria, in the morgue. We once fell asleep on a patient's shoulder while taking her pulse. Unprofessional.

But that wasn't all of it. The endoscopic-equipped operating theater itself, Room 101, normally a significant profit-center for the facility, wasn't profiting from us. Facilities Management had little subtle ways of hassling us, reminding us that other, better-funded patients were having their profit-centered procedures delayed, and that the bottom line was bottoming out, somewhat, in Room 101. Surprise inventory inspections, brownouts, unscheduled sprinkler tests, that sort of thing. Mount Venuda General is supposed to be a teaching hospital, but apparently there are limits. That's why Doctor Spinejack suggested we institute an honorarium.

Q: An honorarium?

A: Yes, a sum. A sliding scale amount, for access. Adjusted for the level of access.

Q: What levels of access did you offer?

A: We offered, basically, external and internal access. Internal was extra.

Q: How much did you charge?

A: The scale slid a great deal. Initially, with the local news stations, we charged less: KPMS, Newscenter Six, Action Team Twelve. Those guys got a steal. But then when Nightline arrived with their whole unit, a great big mobile home with more gear strapped to it than in our entire radiology wing, that's when we jacked the rates. Just as a deterrent, you know, following free-market principles. Increase the cost, we thought, to reduce the demand.

Q: Was the demand reduced by the increased cost?

A: Hell no. There was a line down the block to crawl up that lady's rectum.

Q: Is it true you were the first film and television producer to set foot in the rectum of Agnes Cuddlebottom?

CARL B. JOHNS, EXECUTIVE VICE-PRESIDENT, FAMILY HORIZONS CINEMA:

Well, a lot of people call themselves producers. But I was the first, I guess, to see this on TV and say to myself: that woman's rectum has heart. It has something universal. It's exciting, and it's dramatic. It's a hell of a story. And I just felt I had to be a part of that.

Q: How did you approach Mrs. Cuddlebottom about the rights to her story?

A: Well, obviously she was in no condition to sign anything, the poor woman. We didn't know if she'd live or die, though of course I was rooting for her, and upon her recovery I was sure we'd be able to offer her something significant. And we put out some feelers, just in case, to find any heirs of hers who would need to be paid off. But there were other players, other stories ... Doctor Fokker, of course, was the public face of the operation, making new discoveries every day as he worked his way up the brutal pathway of these ruined, post-apocalyptic intestines. Down at Camp Reno, where the media people had set up their little village, we all waited on pins and needles for every scrap of news, every detail. Fokker was really the hero, I think, that America needed at that hour.

Q: Those were difficult times, at that hour.

A: Very rough times. A really iffy hour. You had the non-localized conflict going on, terrorists blowing up schools, all those dolphins washed up dead on that beach in Malibu, and of course the whole financial mess—the dollar getting raped by the peso, the gas riots, the mortgage riots, all that. Americans were down and out. They didn't think things could get any worse. But then, when people heard about this lady Agnes Cuddlebottom, heard how she'd kicked heroin, escaped from her abusive pimp, started a new life for herself, and then fallen victim to this mystery illness, this, this *thing* in her, that baffled medical science ... people said to themselves: that could have been me. I could have a *thing* in me. It could happen to me, you, anybody.

Q: It definitely could not happen to me. I take precautions.

A: Well, we didn't know then what we know now. The tragic events, as you say, were still folded.

Q: I wrote that line. About the unfolding.

A: Great line, that line.

Q: I do a lot of writing, on the side.

A: Any screenplays?

Q: I have a couple treatments.

A: We should talk later. I'd love to see what you're working on.

Q: I've got this one, it's about this interviewer, he works for this kind of nameless, faceless government entity, and you know, he's an idealist but a workaholic, he's so dedicated to his job that his wife leaves him, so he's very lonely ... and then ... then there's this magical quest, it's kind of complicated, but basically he becomes this hero, sort of, who has to find the location of these crystals ... it's set in the Old West ... there's singing ...

A: Right. Well ...

Q: But we were discussing the tragic events.

A: Okay, yes. First of all, I wouldn't make those tragic events the focus. It would be based on a true story, but you know, we can't end it like that. It needs to be uplifting. Now, more than ever.

Q: Tell me, what was your role at Base Camp?

A: You mean Camp Reno.

Q: Right, I mean Camp Reno.

A: Well first of all I'm the guy who convinced everybody to call it Camp Reno. 'Reno' is trucker slang for the letter R, for Rectum. But more to the point, the name had color. Camp Reno sounds like a place you might want to visit, a place where some action might happen. Base Camp made it sound like the action is all somewhere else. And pretty soon everybody was calling it Camp Reno, so I felt that was a coup.

Q: I agree, Camp Reno is way better.

A: Way. And then also, I was the first guy to say: look, we're all in this thing together, let's pool our resources. Let's get, like, a media resource center, someplace we can work, or just take a coffee break. Some folding chairs, maybe a sofa. Some air fresheners, *please*. Create an environment where we can compare notes, and such. I think I brought a lot of camaraderie to the atmosphere in there, which had been up to that point very tense.

Camp Reno was all news people, at that point in the story. And let me tell you about news people: they're pushy, competitive, they're all after the same story. They hate waiting, they hated being cooped up in that stinky little cave, just waiting most of the time ... and they drink. All of them, they drink like fish. Every one of those reporters has a flask on them someplace. At first it seemed fun, but eventually fights always broke out, and I'd try to just, you know, mediate. Call me crazy, but I think I made a real difference there.

And I'd do the little things. I made the coffee. I watered the ficus. I replaced the cartridges in the injket. But above all I hung on every word, every scrap of news those guys brought back. I just got caught up in the story. That's my job.

ARCHIVAL TRANSCRIPT PROVIDED BY WPMS-23 NEWS ARCHIVES: BRENDA SPONGE REPORTING.

BRENDA SPONGE:

Thanks Tim. I'm talking to you live from the splenic flexure, the very tip-top of the descending colon, and with me is Doctor Emil Muller-Fokker. Doctor Fokker, what's the next step in this exciting operation to rescue Agnes Cuddlebottom?

DR. FOKKER:

Well Brenda, we've had a setback. Ahead of us, as you can see, the distal end of the transverse colon is clenched like a fist. This is due to a colonic stricture at a local point of inflammation, which is a dangerous condition in most colons, but in Mrs. Cuddlebottom colon it's just about par for the course. It's blocking our progress toward the appendix.

BS: Couldn't you use a laxative of some kind? Or maybe blast your way through with explosives?

DF: Unfortunately, no. The patient has already failed to respond to our normal arsenal of general relaxants, and explosives are just too risky. However, the Spinejack Transform gives us a unique opportunity: from this vantage point, we can apply a topical antispasmodic-quaalude cream directly on the contracted tissues, softening them enough that we can squeeze through the stricture and reach the other side. What we'll find there, I don't know.

BS: I see that you and your friend Jojo are wearing full-body latex suits. What's the purpose of that?

DF: Well, by coating ourselves with Pepto-Bismol and quaaludes, we'll simultaneously lubricate our passage through this tight squeeze, and hopefully soften the tissues around us. But such a large topical dose of laxative could be quite embarrassing, or worse, for myself or Jojo.

BS: Embarrassing? What do you mean?

DF: Well … it's a laxative. I have a normal, healthy colon that responds to laxatives, and I ate recently …

BS: Oh! Right! (*Laughter.*) Understood! (*Laughter*) That would, um … ah, (*expletive*) it. We'll have to cut that question. Never mind, let's continue. Wait actually—Sam? Call Gertie and tell her to get me some kind of outfit for this. A diving suit, but it's got to stand out in the light. Something tight and tiny, I wanna show some (*expletive*). Anyway, sorry Doctor—

DF: That's quite all right, Brenda. Are we rolling? Okay.

BS: Doctor Fokker, what awaits us on the other side of this stricture?

DF: Beyond the stricture is the lateral transit of the lower intestine. It ought to be easy going: wide, flat, relatively dry, less gaseous … a nice spot for a romantic weekend getaway!

BS: (*Laughter.*)

DF: (*Laughter.*)

BS: (*Laughter.*)

DF: (*Laughter.*) But seriously, I'm concerned with our rate of progress. Agnes is counting on us to reach this obstruction, and she can't hold on forever. So we've got our work cut out for us. Come on, Jojo! let's grease up!

BS: Where is Jojo going, Doctor?

DF: Jojo? I ... I don't know. Jojo! Come back here! Jojo? Jojo ...

Q: You are the first monkey to set foot inside the rectum of Agnes Cuddlebottom, is that correct?

JOJO THE CHIMP (*signing*):
GIVE JOJO GOLDFISH GOLDFISH.

Q: Of course. Please, help yourself.

A: JOJO EAT LOVE GOLDFISH.

Q: How long did you know Doctors Muller-Fokker and Spinejack before the Cuddlebottom operation?

A: GOLDFISH. GOLDFISH GOLDFISH.

Q: Your friends Emil and Otto? How long did you work together?

A: NO OTTO BAD OTTO. JOJO HATE HATE OTTO. OTTO BAD TOUCH JOJO.

Q: It's okay, Jojo, don't worry, Otto isn't here right now. Otto isn't here.

A: BAD TOUCH. BAD TOUCH OTTO GO DIE. JOJO AFRAID.

Q: No Otto, Jojo, I promise! But what about Emil? Was Emil your friend?

A: JOJO LOVE GOOD EMIL. FOLLOW GOOD GOLDFISH FRIEND. LOVE LOVE.

Q: And did you enjoy the time you spent with your friend Emil in the rectum of Agnes Cuddlebottom?

A: HATE HATE HATE HATE HATE POOP PLACE. BAD STINKY POOP. BAD STINKY POOP NO BANANA TREE. JOJO NO FIND BANANA TREE. FIND BAD STINKY POOP AND BUG. BUG TASTE POOP. NO BANANA. GIVE JOJO BANANA BANANA.

Q: I'm sorry to hear that.

A: GIVE JOJO BANANA BANANA.

Q: But still, you could have turned back, couldn't you? Or did you feel ... coerced?

A: BANANA BANANA BANANA BANANA BANANA BANANA BANANA—

Q: I don't have a banana, Jojo, I'm sorry.

A: JOJO WANT EMIL BANANA GOLDFISH HOME NOW.

Q: I'm sorry, but I have to ask just a few more of these questions.

A: NO. BANANA BANANA.

Q: Can you tell me more about what Otto and Emil—

A: GIVE JOJO BANANA OR EAT POOP.

Q: Can we ... (*whispering*) ... okay Jojo, listen, we'll get you a banana, okay. That lady there is going right now to find a banana for you.

A: WOMAN NO GO POOP PLACE. POOP PLACE NO BANANA. GO SUPERMARKET.

Q: Will you talk to us some more, while we wait for the banana?

A: GOLDFISH.

Q: Why did you run away when your friend Emil entered the colonic stricture?

A: JOJO SMELL BUGS. JOJO AFRAID. JOJO WANT HOME HOME.

Q: But what about your friend, Emil?

A: JOJO SORRY SAD. JOJO NO MORE EAT POOP FOR LOVE FRIEND EMIL. JOJO NEW MOVIE FRIEND GIVE BANANA BANANA BANANA. JOJO LOVE EMIL. EMIL STRONG GOOD. EMIL FIND BANANA TREE FOR JOJO. JOJO AND MOVIE FRIEND FIND MOVIE FOR EMIL. NO MORE POOP PLACE. SORRY SAD SAD.

Q: Or so you thought. But it didn't exactly turn out that way, did it?

A: YOU BAD. JOJO WANT LAWYER FRIEND. JOJO NO TALK. EAT POOP. GO DIE.

TRANSCRIBED EXCERPT FROM THE VOICE RECORDER OF DR. FOKKER:

DF: August 16, 4:31pm ... We made it. It was a harrowing squeeze through the stricture ... the obvious comparisons to a bolus aside, I'm feeling less fecal now, but still recovering from mild symptoms of claustrophobia. Fortunately, there's plenty of space here to stretch and wander around. Miss Sponge is resting against the colon wall, recovering her composure while together we take in this frankly remarkable scene. It's a deep, vast cavity, as large as a football stadium relative to us in our N-space-folded condition. Of course I know this is an artificial, temporary size relationship, but with the faint pink light shining through the dermis and the exterior colon, the entire place resembles some enchanted lagoon at sunset. Glittering translucent polyps dangle overhead, swaying in the breeze and scattering light like thousands of mirrored disco balls. The odor of digestive gases is much less pronounced here, thank goodness. It's a very pleasant surprise. I deeply regret that Jojo isn't with me to see it.

Peering into the shimmering pool of fluid I see a school of bacilli endoteria frolicking just below the surface. These are a common intestinal biota that I've only ever seen on slides before. If I could catch one here it would be nearly as large as my hand! Amazing research opportunities await us in this place, and in colons everywhere, thanks to Doctor Spinejack's discovery.

Miss Sponge is—oh, sorry, excuse me. Miss Sponge is, um, removing her protective gear. She's just asked me if the lagoon is safe for swimming. From what I know of this area of the colon, it should be non-toxic, but we must proceed carefully because— hey! Don't, hey ... oh (*expletive.*) There she goes. Miss Sponge? Miss Sponge! You have to be very careful, please! Please don't just jump in there and ...

(*Giggling. Splashing. Expletives.*)

Miss Sponge ... has just drenched me ... with what tastes like a mild saline solution. I detect no urea or other standard fecal ingredients, thankfully. Nevertheless it's extremely reckless to—

(*Splashing.*)

Brenda! What are you doing? Your epidermis is completely exposed! We can't—

(*Splashing, giggling.*)

Oh! That's it! That! Is! It! You're going to get it, lady! I played water polo at Cal!

(*Voice recorder falls to ground. Giggling, splashing.*)

Hey, cut it out! You're pulling off my ... oh ... heh ...

DF: Hi, me again. It's later on August 16, I'm not sure what time of day ... don't really care. We're just taking a rest, here on the edge of this lake that we're calling Lake Mucosa for now. The epithelial cell layer here is soft and grassy, very nice to lie on. Womb-like. The waves are lapping at our toes. And I'm feeling very peaceful, and very relaxed.

And very (*provocative slang term*) for Brenda Sponge and her (*provocative anatomical term*).

(*Giggling.*)

Which is one of the nicest (*provocative anatomical term*) I've ever (*expletive*).

(*Laughter.*)

Tomorrow is a new day with much to do, but for tonight, this is Doctor Emil Muller-Fokker, signing off from Mucosa Beach, in the transverse colon of Mrs. Agnes Cuddlebottom. Good night.

Q: Is it true you opened the very first Starbucks in the rectum of Agnes Cuddlebottom?

CHESTER BOUFFANT, STARBUCKS FRANCHISEE:
Yes I did. Though it was just a kiosk.

Q: That's sure some outside-of-box thinking.

A: Thanks. It was the natural next step though: I already had going three Starbucks kiosks in the hospital at that time. Cafeteria, main lobby, and cardiology. Cardiology was the closest to the GI wing, and when all these TV people started hanging out over there I got slammed, 'cause I just brew fast enough with just two pots. When I ran out they wouldn't wait for the next pot; they started going across the street, to the Starbucks at the student union. I don't make no money off that, that's one of Henry Conker's Starbucks. They all started drinking them Frappuccinos, and I ain't got no Frappuccinos in a kiosk. I got drip. That bastard Henry Conker was bleeding me dry.

Q: There must have been unique health code issues, serving food in a hospital.

A: Nah. Never saw a health inspector anywhere near the place. I think they're scared of getting sick. So anyway ... I just went for it, ordered up a new kiosk. First I was just gonna set up outside Room 101 there, but when I really thought hard about it, I just knew: you gotta take it to the customer.

Q: Did you obtain any sort of permission from Mrs. Cuddlebottom to operate a Starbucks franchise in her excretory system?

A: Course I did! I mean, I tried to. So, no. But basically yes, because ... thing is, you couldn't get near that lady. With all them doctors and nurses around her, all them guys with the ass-cameras, and all them nut-cases from the public trying to get a glimpse of her, sneaking around the wards, snapping pictures for their internet porno blogs and stealing rubber gloves ... and then what? Then, I see them all drinking Java Chip Frappuccinos and Toffee Nut Lattes *across the street!*

Q: So you never actually spoke to her?

A: How could I? They had her drugged up most the time. Whenever she did wake up they'd just put her back down. But I wrote her this letter, and I pinned it to—

Q: Hang on, excuse me please ... Mrs. Cuddlebottom was in a deep coma, was she not?

A: Look, I just do coffee. Not even that: I just do *drip.* This place is crawling with doctors if you wanna get medical.

Q: But did you ever see her awake?

A: No, I never saw her, but I sure heard her swearing up a blue streak once or twice. How do you think she liked it, being up to her neck in turds with that giant butt trumpet in her ass? Not so much! If I'd been her I'd have been begging for a bullet. So no, you couldn't get near that lady, and if you did she was sleeping, and if she wasn't sleeping she'd just as soon bite your head off as talk to you. It was stressful, sure. It was nuts in that place! Things were a helluva lot better on the inside.

Q: How so?

A: Business boomed! I sold more coffee in a day down
there than in a whole week topside. Hit all my numbers straight
off the bat, even with Doc Otto and his nurse mafia hitting me
up for a cut. Those TV guys drink coffee like it's poon tang. My
regional sales manager was loving it, he bragged and bragged
about the Starbucks in Agnes' ass. He pulled some strings and
we even got Frappuccinos. In a goddamn kiosk! First kiosk ever
with those.

Q: What a quintessential American success story.

A: After that first week I was on cloud nine. It felt like this
fresh frontier down there. Like I was some kind of Daniel Boone
guy. I mean, it was rustic as hell, but everybody loved good
coffee. I got to know people, it had a friendly, small-town feel.
And it let me get away from all the craziness up in the wing. In
the world, even.

Q: The non-localized conflict?

A: Yeah! That, and all the trees dying, and the space junk
hitting people, and them cannibal cops down in L.A., eating
them basketball players, all that. The world was getting scary.
But inside of Agnes, I don't know why but I felt safe and warm.
Crazy, huh? Maybe it helps that I got no sense of smell at all.

Q: Really? None at all?

A: Yeah, cause of an Army thing. I was in one of the
conflicts that used to be localized: the inspections in Kzb,

TRANSCRIBED EXCERPT FROM THE VOICE RECORDER OF DR. MULLER-FOKKER:

DF: August 19th. Early morning. I'm standing at the edge of a deep precipice: the ascending colon, which we must scale on our approach to the appendix. We're past the halfway-point on our journey to the ileum of the small intestine, site of Mrs. Cuddlebottom's obstruction. But this next leg of our trip will be perilous. The decrepitude of the colon wall leaves us with few footholds on a very long, steep slope. Also, due to our continuing progress along the Spinejack Transform, our size continues to reduce relative to the patient. The polyps on the colon wall now rise up like boulders on a rocky landscape. The intestinal biota, which I found adorable before, have grown larger and more fearsome. However, we're obviously not part of their evolved food chain, and they've shown no aggression, so I'm confident they don't pose a threat. In fact one of them, an E. Coli bacterium with long, floppy cilia and a purplish hue, is quite playful and friendly, and he seems to have adopted us. I named him McDermot, and I've taught him to roll over and beg for goldfish crackers. Nevertheless, I recognize now that we should expect a minor but exponential slowing of our progress due to the continued N-space folding. It's difficult to estimate what size we'll be when we reach our surgical goal.

Brenda is giving an interview to Martha Stewart's Assisted Living magazine at the moment, supported by her team of colonoscopic camera operators and Gertie, her endo-sartorial wardrobe mistress.

Privately I must admit some conflict in my feelings for

Brenda. She's a forceful woman, very capable, but headstrong in the extreme. As danger mounts, I worry more and more that she'll do something stupid that might jeopardize the operation. And yet … when we're apart, even for a few moments, I feel a yawning emptiness in my thoracic cavity, and a yearning that stretches from my anterior perineum to the terminus of my urethra. She stimulates my neuroendocrine axis in ways no woman has before. I need her. It's curious how fate brought us together here, of all places. Nevertheless, Brenda believes, and I agree, that we should keep our feelings for each other out of the devouring spotlight of publicity for now. So this recording is filed PERSONAL, and strictly off the record.

Here comes Brenda, and we're ready to begin the climb. I've secured our line to a sturdy outcropping of infected polyps. I'll repel to a halfway point, followed by Brenda, and then— Hi, honey, can you—

(*Loud rumbling. Screams. Sucking, squirting noises. More screams. Louder rumbling. Voice recorder falls to ground.*)

BRENDA SPONGE: Emil!

MCDERMOT: Woof! Woof!

DF: Brendaaaaaaaa! (*Continues for twelve seconds.*) (*Thump.*) Owch! (*Expletive.*) Wup! Wha—(*Thump, grunt.*) (*Expletive.*) Aaaaaaaaa! (*Continues for nine seconds, slowly fades out.*)

BS: Oh God! Camera! Sam, roll that (*expletive*) camera! Turn the light on! Okay, rolling? … Hello America, this is Brenda Sponge! I'm live in the Cuddlebottom Colon, with a chilling update!

Q: As members of the print media, how did you react to the news of Doctor Fokker's sudden jeopardy?

MEMBERS OF THE PRINT MEDIA:
        Ours was a bittersweet reaction. On the one hand, it was great news! Drama! Excitement! Everybody breathlessly awaiting the updates! It's what we live for. The rising tide, you know. It floated our boats.

Q: It's been called "the fart heard around the world."

A: That was us, we called it that! Also: COLON CRISIS! Also: BUTT-TRUMPET TERROR! We had four-color pull-outs, we had website infographics. All that was sweet. But then, bitterness also. Because when you're in print, you always feel scooped by the TV people. They're always first on the scene, in their fancy-pants suits with their fancy-pants news vans. When we started reporting the news back in the day, our equipment was a hat with a press card in it, a tiny pencil, a cup of coffee and a deadline! We are journalists! We deal in depth! We are hardcore! Those TV people deal in lipstick and sound bites. That bimbo Brenda Sponge gets all the sponsorships but she couldn't tell you a thing about the context. That burned us; that itched.

Q: What context do you mean?

A: The danger context! The Times ran a sunday magazine special on everything that could go wrong with this operation, including why the ascending colon is subject to what they call "involuntary contractile reflex." That's what happened: irritate the walls of the intestines too much and they twitch, and you fart, or "flatulate" as our medical guys like to say. It's an inner defense mechanism, a booby-trap. The intestines are full of peril! That's why we called it: RAIDERS OF THE LAST FART! And *that* is what I mean by depth.

Q: Knowing what you did, then, did you ever attempt to warn Doctor Fokker?

A: We warned everybody! All anybody had to do was pay fifty cents for a newspaper, or a buck fifty on a Sunday! We had distribution in there, too. We had a stand in Camp Reno, next to the Starbucks, and then later in Camp Marlin. We were the only people saying anything about the potential for tragic events to unfold. If they'd only listened.

Q: You also reported, I believe, on a Bigfoot sighting in that area.

A: Absolutely! And we provided the context for Bigfoot sightings, gave people the background, gave them the tools to understand. The tools to protect themselves, too, in case Bigfoot ever did show up somewhere. You never know. We might all have Bigfoot in our ass and just not realize it. But who listens to the print media any more? Kids today, they can't even read unless it's spelled wrong on a phone.

Q: There are those who have said that your headline BUTT-TRUMPET TERROR! is an exploitive and immature description of the Spinejack Transform.

A: No, no, you see that's just the constraints of our medium. For headlines to have real punch, we always strive for a small footprint. "Butt", compared to "Rectum", has half as many syllables, 66 percent fewer letters.

Q: Likewise DOCTOR HEADS UP PATIENT'S ASS?

A: That was the Post! They're like that. We would never do that, never say ASS: Even though BUTT costs us a letter. We have standards!

Q: As Squad Leader of the Mount Venuda Fire Department Search & Rescue Team, how did you get entangled in Agnes Cuddlebottom's rectum?

COMMANDER JOCK THRUSTWORTH, MOUNT VENUDA SEARCH & RESCUE:

At 7:05 on the morning of August nineteenth we received a 911 alert for a 2440 up at the hospital—that's an Man-Trapped-In-Hole situation. I led a team there to assess. We had just done another Man-In-Hole ten days earlier, so we had all the gear for that on the truck already. We deployed in record time, but soon recognized that 2440 was not the correct situation code for that particular situation.

Q: I imagine there was no existing code for that.

A: Yes and no. We're trained on a whole set of Man-Trapped codes. 2400 is just "Man Trapped", so you could use that. There's also 2423, Man-Trapped-In-Sewer, which kind of fit; also 2472, Man-Trapped-In-Carnivour. But it's true, every situation is different. We had to use a creative approach. Fortunately, we had the complete support of everybody at the hospital. Doctor Spinejack was particularly helpful with getting us access.

Q: What kind of access did you need?

A: Well, the Rescue Hummer is the command center for all our Search & Rescue Operations, so locating that vehicle in the operating theater was essential. At 7:19am we established an emergency breach point off the hallway there, and then backed the hummer up the hall to Room 23. We made a smaller emergency breach in the hallway there so we could run a hose out to a hydrant, in case of fire. Doctor Spinejack gave us clearance for those. And then we had to disperse some crowds, in order to do our job, and he was completely supportive.

Q: Are those the crowds that formed when you drove your truck through the hospital wall?

A: Yes. The emergency breach procedure sometimes draws undue attention. It's controversial, but it saves lives. In our job, every second counts! There were quite a few individuals camped outside the hospital at that point. Not just the news people with their vans and their inflatable studios, but also the refugee contingent. Keep in mind, MVS&R spent the previous week dealing with refugees from Hurricane Zorro and Hurricane Yogi, and the cleanup from Hurricane XXX. We had a population of displaced persons moving into the Tri-County area seeking shelter and higher ground, and in some cases medical assistance. Some of them were waving signs about Agnes Cuddlebottom and Doctor Fokker, generally in support, and other people were grilling hot dogs next to their trucks, sunbathing, what have you. So we shot off a couple canisters of crowd dispersal agent right outside the hospital wing, to keep those citizens out of harm's way.

Then, after my men and I got the low-down from Doctor Spinejack on the nature of the terrain, we suited up with full climbing gear, med-kit, emergency oxygen and the Jaws of Life. At 7:24, 17 minutes after deployment, we hit the rectum, hard.

Q: What was your first impression of the rectal situation?

A: Inside? Squalor. The lower rectum area was just

disgusting. People had been urinating and defecating there, tossing their empty coffee cups there, beer cans, cigarette butts ... also there were extension cords and cables of all kinds running through, and a couple of garden hoses, all tangled up together in there, along with a rope ladder someone had made out of surgical tubing and splints. You had your burn hazard, your shock hazard, your slip/fall ... code violations everywhere. It was a death-trap! But we got past it with a couple of forty-foot extension ladders and made it to the sigmoid area by 7:28.

Up in the colon: same deal. A total shanty-town. We issued a half dozen citations right there and then. I tell you it's lucky we got there when we did. That place was going to go up in flames.

Q: Did you encounter problems penetrating the colonic stricture?

A: Not too much trouble—the media beat us to the site, so we gave a couple interviews, and then deployed the Jaws Of Life—a hydraulic jack system we use for a 2402, Man-Trapped-In-Burning-Skyscraper—and once we squeezed out an ADA-sized opening, we installed the Tunnel Of Safety—a quick-curing concrete support system, developed by the Navy for undersea evacuations. There were some slight tremors, but the forms held, and by 8:45AM we had a semi-permanent access route with lighting, non-skid floors, wheelchair access and grounded power outlets every fifteen feet. On the other side we found Brenda Sponge and a couple other TV news people, with their camera men and their hair people and their teeth people, about nine of them in all.

Q: They must have been happy to see you.

A: I'd expect so ... however, several of their colleagues from

105

the print media tailed us during the rescue operation. Ms. Sponge called one of them a sort of name. I think she was under some stress.

Q: A name? What name exactly?

A: Well, not a nice name.

Q: Can you be more specific?

A: Really not nice. If I recall correctly ... she called him an individual who uses his sexual organ as a tool to remove human residue from part of a piece of equipment that's known to be a vector for bacterial infection, and having uncertain parentage.

Q: I see.

A: He, in turn, referred to her as a female dog, also of uncertain parentage, infected with a venereal disease, and likened her surgical breast augmentation to an emergency floatation device. It got worse from there. I immediately identified a classic situation 1635: Brewing Street-Fight. It took some really disciplined, even-handed Tasing to prevent unnecessary violence. But that's also part of our training.

Q: How then did you proceed?

A: We lit off some flares just before 9 AM, hauled in a couple of Ski-Doos and left the rest of the team on crowd control while two of us, myself and First Lieutenant Birch Mattock, tore ass across that lake as fast as gas could get us there.

Q: Sounds like fun.

A:. I'll admit to enjoying that part of the mission, yeah. The roar of the motor, the sea spray in your face ... I guess I'm just a Ski-Doo junkie. And I love my job. So did Birch ...

Q: Is something the matter?

A: No, sorry. Just dry lenses. Anyway, we hit the beach and ran to the point where Doctor Fokker had last been seen, the precipice at the edge of the ascending colon. We dropped some more flares down there, but saw nothing. No answers to our megaphones. No tugs on the String Of Life, when we dangled the String Of Life. Nothing at all. We feared for the worst. So we drew straws, and Birch ... Birch got the short straw ... excuse me ...

Q: Are you crying?

A: No, I've just got something in my eye.

Q: You're crying for your lost comrade?

A: Search and Rescue never cries!

Q: It's okay to cry. We understand. Go ahead and let it out.

A: I'm not crying, goddamit! I just need some saline!

Q: It's difficult for strong men to cry sometimes. Sometimes, when I'm driving home, listening to the Adult Contemporary station I hear that song, "Oooooo Eeeeee, Wa Wa Wa Baby," and it seems like it was written about my first marriage, and I just—

A: I'm not here to cry for you! I'm delivering a report, at

107

the request of this committee! On the unfolding tragedy! That took the life of Birch Mattock! And, and ... goddammit, I need Kleenex! Stat! And 20 ccs of saline! Where's my backup?

UNIDENTIFIED SEARCH & RESCUE OFFICER:
Here, sir! Kleenex! Saline!

A: Good man! Now get back! I'm going to blow my nose!

UNIDENTIFIED SEARCH & RESCUE OFFICER:
Every-body! Get down on the floor! Now! Now!

A: Three! Two! One! Aaaaa-

(Rugged sneezing.)

A: Okay, crisis averted. Return to your stations ... where were we?

Q: Birch Mattock.

A: Birch ... helluva man, he was. Sometimes I wish it was me who drew that short straw. But Birch knew the risks, and he never flinched. He never cried, either. We drove some Spikes-Of-Life into the colon floor, set an anchor and a backup, Birch cinched up his harness, we high-fived, and I belayed him down. We were in radio contact when it happened, at a depth of about 325 feet of climbing rope.

Q: What happened.

A: The Butt Snake! It gobbled him up!

Q: Let's go to audio of that, can we?

108

AUDIO TRANSCRIPT OF LEIUTENANT BIRCH MATTOCK'S PERSONAL "BLACK-BOX" RECORDING SYSTEM DURING ALLEGED GOBBLING BY ALLEGED BUTT SNAKE:

BM: Hey, something's pulling my—WAAAAA!

(Screaming. Struggling. Snapping and popping. Chewing. Spurting of blood from holes. More screaming. Desperate pleas for help. More spurting of blood. More snapping. Chewing, crunching. Agonized whimpers. Coughing of blood. Muffled pleading. More chewing. Choking sound. Wet, ripping sounds. Prayer. Gasping. Coughing. Shuddering More chewing. Occasional twitching. Chewing. Crunching. Chewing. Slithering ...)

TRANSCRIPT FROM THE VOICE-RECORDER OF DR. FOKKER:

DF: Fokker here. I was unconscious, not sure how long ... I've got some rib trauma, potential mild concussion ... no paralysis ... my limbs are mobile, my head and neck are mobile ... I'm damn lucky.

I took quite a tumble. Estimates of distance have become increasingly unreliable due to the Transform, but it seemed an eternity. Now I've come to rest on a round, padded ledge of contractile muscle just opposite the ileo-cecal valve, overlooking the broad flatland of the cecum, the cul-de-sac at the root of the large intestine, gateway to the appendix. McDermot has tracked me here, he's licking my face ... down boy!

It's a peaceful place ... there's a lazy herd of bifidobacteria down there, gnawing on fungi in the shade of a large calcified tumor. A cool, dry wind whispers in my ears. A slow thrum, the distant beating of Agnes Cuddlebottom's heart, reminds me that I must carry on. I seem to be able to stand.

Brenda must be pathologically concerned about me. I hope the stress doesn't aggravate her acute menstrual cramps. I need to leave her some sort of message, to let her know I'm still alive. I'll try to carve my initials in the lumen wall, using one of these long jagged shards of crystalized mineral deposit that are scattered all around this area. I'm very lucky I didn't fall on one of these. Hard, whitish, translucent, slightly irregular ... most curious. I'll take a sample for later study, but for now, it seems to do a good job of leaving visible marks in this soft tissue. E ... F. Seven incisions. I hope someone sees it.

Interesting ... I've noticed, and extracted, a two-inch long shard of this crystal jammed in my left medial thigh. The bleeding isn't severe, but it's puzzling that I feel no pain symptoms at all. The leg presents no numbness otherwise, it's strong, flexible ... tough. Really I feel pretty good. I'll just bandage this up ... yes, I'm lucky to be alive. Ha! What a feeling! The human body is amazingly rugged and ... sexy. I wish Brenda was here to see just how tough I am.

Okay! Yes! It's time to get this mission moving. Yeah! I need to make it to that big ol' ileo-cecal valve over there, and move on up through the small intestine. I'm close, damn close. If I sidle clockwise along this ledge, I should get there within the hour. Okay, I'm moving out! Yes, sir! C'mon, McDermot!

Movin' ... movin' on out ... don't mess around ...

(Doctor Fokker humming "Situation" by Yazoo.)

(Doctor Fokker whistling "We Are The Champions" by Queen.)

(Doctor Fokker singing "Bohemian Rhapsody", ibid.)

Q: At what point did you realize Agnes Cuddlebottom's cecum was full of crystalized cocaine?

CARL B. JOHNS, EXECUTIVE VICE-PRESIDENT, FAMILY HORIZONS CINEMA:

I was, literally, the very last person to find out about this. Sure, I had early possession of the, the stones ... the crystals ... the deposits, if you will—

Q: The cocaine.

A: But I didn't know that! Call me naive, but all I knew was that these rocks made everyone in Camp Marlin feel good about themselves. It brought us closer. It was like magic.

Q: How did you get the cocaine up from the cecum?

A: That was all Jojo's doing. I never once suggested it.

Q: Jojo the Monkey has testified that you traded him bananas for rocks of pure cocaine.

A: That is a total mis-characterization of our relationship! You have to understand, Jojo was hungry to get back in the story. When the rescue guys arrived, and all that action happened ... Jojo felt he should have been there. He knew he had to go after his friend. That's true courage. And also, he had a score to settle with a low-down paramecium named McDermot. Something about that guy didn't seem to square up.

Q: Jojo the Monkey has also testified that he blacked out after you gave him a beverage, and woke up on the cecum floor stuffed inside a duffel bag.

A: In my business we call that Advancing the Arc. He thanked me later.

Q: Weren't you, or Jojo, concerned about this alleged Butt-Snake?

A: I knew Jojo could handle himself. He's a champion, that guy. There's nothing he wouldn't do for a friend, and some bananas.

Q: Your production assistant, Jimmy, has testified that on more than ten occasions he smuggled bananas through the anus for you, hiding them in the legs of his—

A: Wait a minute: *smuggled*, you say? We're *smugglers* now? I ask you, since when is it a crime to bring bananas into some old lady's rectum?

Q: In Texas this was outlawed in 1913.

A: Okay, look ... the rules, clearly, had changed. This was a whole new world. A whole new *jurisdiction!* You could not climb up that ladder in that poor woman's rectum and look out over Camp Reno and think you were still in Texas. Anyway, my focus was elsewhere. My story was unfolding beautifully, studios were calling me, I had distribution lined up, I had Tom Hanks interested, lights were turning green ... I was high on success.

Q: And cocaine.

A: Well, maybe we all were, in a contact-high kind of way. They were burning chunks of it down at the shore, just to freshen the air a little.

Q: And by "they", you mean ...

A: Everybody. Camp Marlin—I named it that, by the way, when I saw one of those big silver bugs jump up out of the water —is where all the long-term embedded people relocated after the tunnel was built. That included myself and my assistant, Jojo and his assistant, about a dozen from the rescue team, one guy running the Starbucks—it was just a kiosk, back then, but he also sold cigarettes, video tape, batteries, condoms, things like that— and about fifty news people. And all their assistants. Just about everybody had an assistant, to run out and fetch camping supplies or lumber or take-out ... whatever we needed.

Q: Bananas?

A: Bananas, goldfish, sure. And before you say anything else: yes, those assistants were children. They were refugee kids, kids who lost their families in the hurricanes, or in the Wal-Mart bombings, or to the meteor strikes. A bunch of them lived in the parking lot outside the hospital. My heart went out to those little guys. They would sneak into the GI wing, pleading for work ... Doctor Spinejack took pity on them, and granted them in and out privileges, in exchange, I think, for some very small fraction of their pay. He didn't have to do that, you know. He could have gotten in real trouble for that.

Q: Oh, he did.

A: But please don't blame those kids. They were just trying to get by in a cruel world.

Q: By selling your cocaine.

A: It's Not! My! Cocaine! Understand? It's Agnes Cuddlebottom's fucking cocaine! She snorted it! Her body dumped it there, secreted it, however. I had no idea, absolutely no idea, how it got there, what it was, or that any of this was happening. All I knew was, the kids loved Jojo, and Jojo loved the kids. Jojo searched for Emil, and he brought back these pretty rocks. The kids traded bananas for Jojo's rocks. It was a game to them, like Pokémon. Jojo got bananas, the kids got rocks, and as Jojo's manager I got cash. Frankly I felt it was high time I got some kind of economic appreciation for everything I'd done down there. Running the media center was not cheap, you know. Inkjet cartridges alone nearly bankrupted me, in the beginning.

Q: So you got your cut, Doctor Spinejack got his cut, Jojo got a cut ... but what about Agnes?

A: What about her? We were trying to save her life! Is that not enough?

TRANSCRIPT FROM THE VOICE-RECORDER OF DR. FOKKER:

DF: Fokker here, wending my way through the dense ileal undergrowth of the distal small intestine. It's very hot here, hot and damp. The microvilli rise on all sides of me like vast tropical trees, with microflora and fungi covering every surface and hanging down in loose clumps. Unidentified bacteria and virii chatter and click all around me as they slither through the undergrowth or swing from vine to vine. It's slow going here, hacking through the spirochettes and fungal threads with my Diggler machete, but according to my GPS unit we're almost at the site of the mysterious blockage, the clog which our external technology could not image.

    McDermot is my forward scout, sniffing on up ahead with his sensitive cillia. But wait! He's stopped ... what is it, McDermot? What do you see?

    Why, hello! Are these your friends?

    We've met a pack of E. Coli, similar in appearance to McDermot, but larger and fluffier. He seems to be on friendly terms with them. McDermot and the other bacteria are sniffing each other's pilli, frolicking, wagging their rear flagella with excitement. They're excruciatingly cute together.

    Now McDermot and the largest of the E. Coli appear to be exchanging genetic material through their blastulae ... communicating ... and now that big bacterium is coming closer, investigating me.

    Hello there. Hell-lo. What's your name? What's your name? My, aren't you large! Large and orange! Yes! That's right!

Maybe I should call you Garfield! Garfield, do you like goldfish? Here, try one ... yes? You like that? Okay, one more—no, first lie down. Lie down, Garfield. No, lie down—hang on, not yet, lie down—No! No! Bad Garfield, no—hey! Let go! OW! OW! Let go, damn it!

Fine, okay, okay ... Jesus Christ! Bad Garfield!

The large E. Coli just ripped my motivational treat pouch right off my fanny pack! I must remember to be very careful. These creatures are cute, but they're huge, and strong, and there's many of them—whoops! Woah, hey, hey ... the pack is surrounding me ... they're lifting me up on their backs ... they're taking me somewhere ... They won't let me free! There's too many of them! Where are we going? Where are you taking me? McDermot, where are you? Brenda! Jojo! HELP!

Q: You were the first property developer to sell time-share condominiums in the transverse colon of Agnes Cuddlebottom, is that correct?

VICTOR A. SCHLECHTBAUER, PRINCIPAL, GRIND-STONE CAPITAL GROUP:

I believe so, yes. There may have been other deals in the works at that time, but we were the first to offer vacation ownership in the Camp Marlin area.

Q: Where did you get a crazy idea like that?

A: It's a very interesting story. I first heard of Lake Mucosa when our site-services subsidiary, Daisy-Fresh Privacy Cubicles, was hired by the staff of Mount Venuda University to bring on-site sanitary services to the Camp Marlin area. Mrs. Cuddlebottom's operation was very big in the news at the time, as you may recall, and our workers came back from there with these amazing stories, just unbelievable stuff. One fellow, Homer, insisted he would move his family there. And at the time I would have agreed with you, that sounded crazy.

Then, fate intervened. My Panamanian golf trip was cancelled at the last minute due to some local bloodshed down there, that whole chupacabra outbreak if you recall. So I was literally stuck on the runway, in the jet with my girlfriend Darla, and Champ, her pug, and my personal assistant Florio, with nowhere to go, wondering how the hell we could salvage the weekend. And I said, what the hell? Let's go meet this famous asshole.

Q: What were your first impressions?

A: I knew Daisy Fresh would sell a lot of cubicles, that's for sure. *(Laughter.)* But seriously, I saw awful things. Just a terrible mess. Chaos, waste, garbage ... a tragedy of the colons, if you will. The sigmoid region had developed a bad homeless problem. I saw strung-out children begging for change, I saw refugees roasting bacteria on a spit over pyres of burning Starbucks cups. But then, when I looked a little harder, I saw something else. Energy. Human potential, waiting to be unleashed. I saw a bustling local economy. I saw growth. I saw cheap, plentiful labor. I saw street lights, mailboxes. I saw septic systems, families, communities ... and then, when Florio pulled our rickshaw through that tunnel, and out into the vastness of the transverse colon ... there I was struck by a vision, a vision that just about gave me a nosebleed! I saw a bright, bright, beautiful future. I saw kids water-skiing, retired couple on paddle-boats, Native Americans fishing and harvesting wild rice. I saw luxury watercraft, floating restaurants, friendly dolphins, a whole vacation paradise on the shores of that beautiful lake. And I wanted it. I wanted it for myself, sure ... but I also wanted to sell it to other people. People just like me.

Q: That's quite a dream.

A: It's just my special take on the world. It's what makes me a developer. Everywhere I look, I see possibilities. I can't help it. Even just looking at your face right now, I can see golf courses, wineries, a ski slope ... maybe some wild game reserves ... a post office .. chairs ...

Q: But Rome wasn't built in a day.

A: Indeed not. And I knew we had to start with the basics.

Sanitary services. Potable water. Internet.

Q: Establishing ownership, property lines, et cetera.

A: Ownership of the sigmoid colon is a surprisingly complex issue.

Q: I would think it's a simple case of Agnes Cuddlebottom owns all of it.

A: One might think that, but when a person is in an persistent vegetative state—

Q: She woke up long enough to call you a crack bastard, for the record—

A: I'm talking hypothetically here. *If* a person is in an persistent vegetative state—or assuming we, in good faith, believe them to be in such a state, and who didn't at the time?—then the execution of their affairs, absent any sort of living will or directives, naturally falls to family members, next of kin, who are themselves empowered to enter into contractual agreements, on the behalf.

Q: Who did you dig up?

A: That's another very interesting story. Agnes Cuddlebottom's family tree is gnarly, with many stumps. Cuddlebottom is not her birth name, but a name given to her by the proprietress of a brothel in Alabama. Her birth certificate reads Agnes Monroe Delilah Jackson Mississippi. Her mother's name was Hallelujah Chorus Mississippi, and her father is listed as John J. Johnson. Agnes had two half-brothers by the same mother. One of them, Jethro Mississippi, rose to the rank of yeoman in the United States Navy before an unfortunate death by friendly fire at Iwo Jima. He left no children. The other, Hankum "Lawless" Mississippi, was stabbed to death in an Alabama prison, where he was incarcerated for conspiracy to prostitute. He also left no children, but his common-law wife at the time of his death, Lorraine De Milo, went on to re-marry and bear a son.

Q: His common-law wife?

A: Yes, the foremost of his common-law wives at the time of death. On his deathbed, Hankum remembered Lorraine as his "first lady," and willed to her his sharpened toothbrush and other effects. That makes Lorraine's son, Joshua Hankum De Milo Sanchez Jr., the half-cousin-in-common-law, and only living relative, of Agnes Cuddlebottom.

Q: So you paid him off.

A: Unfortunately, severe mental retardation from childhood lead paint consumption prevents Mr. Sanchez from executing contracts in the state of Texas. His power of attorney falls to his caregivers, Open Heart and Hands Charities of Plainfield, Alabama. Let me tell you, they have a truly loving, generous and caring group of volunteers there. It warms my heart that Grindstone Capital was able to partner with them, and improve Joshua's quality of life.

Q: How much did that set you back?

A: I'm not at liberty to discuss those details. And honestly, there's things in life you can't put a price on.

Q: Such as vacation property in a dying woman's colon?

A: The market prices that, not me. About eighty dollars per square foot was the high-water mark for that. Assuming certain public contributions, mind you. Assuming power, septic, internet, trash pickup, and of course roads.

Q: Roads?

Q: You actually drove a cement truck up Agnes Cuddle-bottom's rectum?

SEAMUS FLANNAGAN, MIX OPERATOR, HARD-WAY CONCRETE OF VENUDA:
Many is the time I did sir, yeah. I am a driver of cement trucks generally.

Q: The Spinejack Device must have been much larger than I understood.

A: I do believe they did an upgrade at some point, sir, before the tarmac guys came in. I do recall a sign that said GRAND RE-OPENING or some such thing, after they laid that road.

Q: This road led from where to where, exactly?

A: Basically you get off Interstate 10 at exit 37; you take the Alameda cut-off west, about nine miles; you turn right at the Stop & Save; you carry on up Venuda Pass until you get to the Mount Venuda Emergency Medical Driveway, just past the Red Robin there; you make a left, pay the parking guy twenty bucks, cash only; drive around the back; then back it up through the anus, up a steep one-lane switchback, then when it levels out you keep going, until you get to a large parking area that they call Camp Parking. Past that you couldn't fit a cement truck, so we had to use a slurry pump.

Q: Didn't you find it odd, unsettling ... disagreeable ...

anything like that?

A: I got an out-of-range surcharge for them trips, sir. I
found that just dandy. Also I got double-time for working the
pump, 'cause OSHA says it's a two-guy operation, and I'm both
guys. I found that dandy too. Highly dandy. And I also found,
you know, some good bargains on some stuff that's real expensive
in the neighborhoods I usually get it in. Medicine I mean. For
my nose problems.

      So no, I gotta say I had no complaining to do at that
point in time. Hard on the clutch, I could say, but whatever. It's
not my truck, I just drive it.

ARCHIVAL TRANSCRIPT PROVIDED BY WPMS-23 NEWS ARCHIVES: BRENDA SPONGE REPORTING.

(Very loud chopping of helicopter blades.)

BRENDA SPONGE:
Hello America! I'm Brenda Sponge! And this is: "Operation Cuddlebottom! Deep Impact!"
(Theme music: "Theme From Cuddlebottom")
I'm speaking to you live! From a C-13 Search and Rescue Chopper! And we are landing, right now, in the notorious cecum! Of Agnes Cuddlebottom! The site! Of a grisly attack! That left one man dead! And another! Anal explorer Doctor Emil Muller-Fokker! Missing!

With me are! Commander Jock Thrustworth! Of Mount Venuda Search and Rescue! And his crack team! Of rescue marines!

COMMANDER JOCK THRUSTWORTH:
Semper Fi!

BS: And our guide! Who you all know well! Jojo! The monkey!

JOJO THE MONKEY (SIGNING):
EAT POOP.

BS: Jock! We're almost down! What's the scenario?

JT: Our pilot has fogged the area with Lysol. On my signal, we deploy and secure the cecum! Any signs of resistance, and my rescuers will shoot to kill!

BS: This is personal for you! Isn't it, Jock!

JT: For all of us, Brenda. We lost one of our best men down here. All right boys ... hit it hard!

SEARCH AND RESCUE MARINES (CHORUS):
      Semper Fi!

(Scuffling, grunting.)

BS: Jojo! What dangers lurk! In this extreme action zone! Of the colon!

JOJO (SIGNING):
      FIND EMIL. MAKE MOVIE. EAT BANANA. GO HOME.

(Helicopter blade chopping slows ...)

BS: Let's get a camera out there! For a first glimpse of this eerie alien landscape! The brave men of Mount Venuda Search and Rescue are fanning out ... lighting flares ... look! There, about a hundred meters ahead of us, there's a group of creatures! They're roughly the size and shape of sheep, they're semi-transparent, and they're covered in long wriggling hairs that seem to scintillate. They must be intestinal bacteria of some kind, the Gut Flora, huddled together beside a rocky outcropping. Are they aware of us? Are they friend or foe? Are they watching us, just waiting for their chance to ... good lord!
      Napalm! The MVSR Marines are napalming the

enemy bacteria ... oh my goodness ... they're burning right up ... I saw no aggression, but ... oh dear, they're writhing on the cecum floor, all of them ... folks, this is antibacterial warfare at its most brutal ... the cecum is filling with a thick, sweet-smelling smoke, and now the men are—oh! Bayonets! They're stabbing and re-stabbing the burning ... enemies ... well this is certainly a thorough procedure. Make no mistake, when Mount Venuda Search and Rescue sets out to save lives, they ... aw *(expletive)*. Okay, we'll be right back with more of "Operation Cuddlebottom: Deep Impact!"

Commercial? Good! Christ, I can't believe this *(expletive)*. Follow me, this is going to be hard-hitting!
(Scuffling, stomping of shoes on cecum floor.)
You there! You men! Stop urinating on that burning bacteria! That is sick! That is just un-called-for! Jock, what are they doing?

JT: Brenda, go wait in the chopper.

BS: Wait in the chopper hell! You just napalmed a bunch of innocent—

JT: They're bacteria, Brenda! They don't matter. You've do worse every time you bleach your panties.
(Loud slap.)

JT: Brenda ... you're so hot when you're angry.

BS: Oh Jock ... you're such a bastard! But what's this smoke everywhere?

JT: It smells like victory to me! Whaddya say to that, boys?

(*SEARCH AND RESCUE MARINES:* disciplined whooping.)

BS: This smoke smells ... *(sniffing)* ... familiar. Heh ... *(deep sniffing)* I kind of like it, hmmm.

(Deep sniffing, heavy breathing.)

JT: Kiss me, baby!

(Smooching. Laughter. Huffing.)

CAMERA: All riiiiight, Brenda? We're back on ... in five! Four!

MARINE: Sir, should we put out this fire?

CAMERA: Three! Two!

JT: Ha ha! Let it burn!

MARINES: (Laughter)

BS: (Laughter)

(Loud spank.)

BS: Oww! You ... wouldn't believe what we've just seen here, America. I'm Brenda Sponge, reporting live from the cecum of Operation Cuddlebottom: Deep Impact!

(Theme music.)

BS: This brave team from Mount Venuda Search and Rescue has just disinfected the cecum area, and the mood is festive. The men are exchanging high-fives, chest-bumping ... there's some homo-erotic posturing—

MARINE: Semper Fi!

BS: —all in good fun, of course. Tell me, Commander Jock Thurstworth, what's the next stage in this operation? How do we build on this success, going forward?

JT: We remain vigilant, Brenda! Always watchful! My men are sweeping the area for any trace of—

MARINE: Sir! We've found something! A bloody bandage!

BS: A bandage ... Doctor Fokker! He was trained in the use of bandages!

JT: This tells me he was alive when he got here. Probably stitched himself up and forged ahead. I know that's what I'd do.

BS: But ahead to where did he forge?

JT: We can only assume he went deeper. According to this map Doctor Spinejack sold us in the Visitor's Center, there should be an opening, somewhere above us ... I see it. There! That big squinty hole!

BS: The ileo-cecal valve!

(Music sting!)

JT: We'll have to blast through it. Ready the Lax-Cannon!

MARINE: Lax-Cannon armed, sir!

BS: Lax-Cannon? That sounds serious!

JT: It's a surface-to-surface muscle relaxant delivery system we designed for this mission. It mount on a standard Army T.O.W. missile. Masterson over there guides it to the target with those goggles, and relaxation is assured. Ready, Masterson?

MASTERSON: Ready sir!

JT: Don't worry, it's medical. Though it might sting a little ... fire the Lax-Cannon!

(Whoosh ... loud explosion.)

MASTERSON: Direct hit, sir! Semper Fi!

BS: Look! The valve! It's opening!

JOJO: Chee! Chee! Screep screep! Eeee eee aa aa aa! Screep!

BS: Jojo? Wait! Where are you going?

JT: Stop him! He's got our map!

BS: No! Hold your fire! He's just a monkey!

JT: He's climbing into to the valve ... what's he doing up there? What is he saying?

JOJO (SIGNING):
        GO HOME NOW! NOW, NOW, NOW, GO HOME!
        POOP PLACE BAD, BAD, BAD.
        YOU BIG, STUPID MAN: BAD!
        YOU BIG, STUPID WOMAN: BAD!
        MAN WOMAN HIT HURT POOP PLACE. POOP
PLACE BIG. MAN WOMAN SMALL, SMALL, SMALL.

POOP PLACE KILL YOU, KILL JOJO. STUPID MAN WOMAN STAY, DIE AND EAT POOP! NO JOKE! JOJO FIND EMIL. JOJO BRING EMIL HOME. MAN WOMAN GO KISS IN CAR, IN HOUSE, AIRPLANE, TOILET, JOJO NO CARE. GO. GO GO GO!

NO LIE NO JOKE. JOJO NO TALK POOP. GO OR DIE.

WAIT HOME FOR JOJO. GOOD MAN. GOOD WOMAN. JOJO BRING BANANA.

Q: Tell me about the Agnes Cuddlebottom Concerts For Peace.

**STIFF SUDDENLY, EVENT PROMOTER, GUITARIST/
SINGER FOR EMI RECORDING GROUP "BOHEMIAN
ONSLAUGHT":**
Well man, you gotta remember the times. It was super-heavy out there. Super-fuckin-heavy.

Q: Heavy out where?

A: Outside of Agnes. Everywhere, I mean. Shit was just going to hell. All those people who died in that earthquake, remember that? And all those people who ate all the people who died? That was fierce. And then they all died too! Poisoned, by the dudes they ate. Not cool!

Q: You're talking about the Cincinnati Beef Riots.

A: Yeah, but that's just for instance! That's just one thing, right? Then there were all those refugees from Hurricane Summer, living in parking lots, eating raccoons, getting stung up by killer bees. And then the non-localized conflict got all severe. Democrats and Republicans, shooting at each other, dividing up neighborhoods. And meanwhile, downloaders were just killing the music market! Not just our band, either. Every other band we toured with was all: woah! This sucks! We're all going broke!
  I mean, in retrospect maybe it wasn't all that bad, maybe it seems like you could be nostalgic for it now. But at

the time I was just saying: Stop the world! I want off! I want to transfer to a different world! One that's going uptown, instead of downtown! Can I do that? Is my transfer valid? Do I have to, like, tear the little tab off my transfer? And what does that even mean? I just didn't know, man. That's what "Stuck in a Downtown World" is all about: exactly that feeling.

But that other world, man. That uptown world. That's where everybody wanted to be. And Agnes symbolized that. Agnes and her magic butt.

Q: But why hold a music festival in a dying woman's colon?

A: It was the place to be, man. A hot new scene. And nobody had done that, ever. We were like, pioneers! Bringing the power of music to a new land, messengers of positive energy. I just knew it would help her get better, you know. I'm not a doctor exactly, but I'm a musician, which is similar, and I believe in the healing power of music.

And when I finally got up the nerve to talk to people about this freaky butt-concert idea of mine ... amazingly, people got behind it, they loved it! As soon as we announced the shows, man, it was like Fate, how it all fell into place. Sponsors lined up, vendors lined up, everyone wanted to help. Everyone wanted to play, too. We had to, like, get kind of exclusive about the bill and who was on it. Even with three stages.

Q: Did you foresee, when you announced the concerts, the mass migration of humanity to follow?

A: No way, man! I mean, it was cool and all, but I think maybe we would have charged more. Supply and demand, you know. 'Cause this was supposed to be a charity concert, to help out the refugees, and Agnes, and, you know, peace is expensive. But we barely broke even.

Q: How much did you charge?

A: Well it was supposed to be sliding scale, but the gate people, at the hospital, they said twenty bucks a head. So it was twenty bucks plus sliding. We hardly made anything off the gate. But T-shirts did well, and bandanas. And Grindstone built the stages and the parkway and all that, totes gratis, plus they gave us a killer deal on the toilets. 'Cause they believe in peace too. People who clean toilets, dude, are some of the most spiritual people you'll ever meet. I wish I could be more like them.

Q: How many people attended the Concerts for Peace?

A: On the first day, man, literally three-quarters of a million people! It was a zoo. I never saw anything like it, and I'm almost twenty-eight. B.O. opened, you know, and it was so much bigger than our biggest show ever. And that huge, huge crowd was hella generous with their love, and their attention, and with not throwing shit, and not stabbing each other, and just being cool. Which was super-important because security was all: Hey Dude, there's three-quarters of a million dudes over there and, like, fifty of us dudes. And dude, we're shitting our pants.

But then, you gotta realize that for every person who came in, there were some number of other people sitting out there in the refugee camps, watching the shows on those video walls we set up. 'Cause those people were suffering, you know. Nobody needed the healing power of music more than they did. Even if they couldn't afford to actually come inside.

Q: At what point did the National Guard get involved?

A: Day two. It was a crazy situation, you know? We tried to bulk up security, but, remember, ManBlastah and Hoobestank were headlining! Even after we closed the gates officially, about

134

another hundred thousand fans snuck in somehow. Bribed the doctors or I don't know how, there was something sketchy going on there for sure. We were getting nervous, everything was hella stretched. So some of our people talked to some guys who knew some dudes who knew the President, and we worked a deal where, yes, it's an official State of Emergency, but also it's still a Concert for Peace. We were totes clear about that. And they promised us, assured us, that it would be mellow. There would be no tear gas, no rubber bullets, no, like, Taser tanks electrocuting people in the refugee camps, none of that stuff. The National Guard would just hang out, and, you know, keep the Peace. We had high-level assurances of mellowness.

Q: You're saying the President lied to you.

A: That mo-fo burned us, big time! Taser tanks? Everywhere! Fucking hailstorm of rubber bullets! But all of that went down outside, though. At Cuddlebottom Arena, the mellowness held. I didn't hear about the deaths at first, because ManBlastah was ripping it up on stage , absolutely shredding, and I was focused on my buzz. But then ... then came the bum-rush.

Q: Just how many people did you expect to fit up one human rectum, Doctor Spinejack?

DR. OTTO SPINEJACK:
N people, where N, in theory, is an unlimited number. In theory, the gastro-intestinal tract of Agnes Cuddlebottom could have provided a warm, safe refuge for all of mankind. A new beginning, if you will. The only practical limitation on N being the strength of the N-dimensional Impedance Transform Intersection, and the power of the computing systems that organize it. We strove constantly to improve the throughput of this.

Q: What did you do with all the money, Doctor Spinejack?

A: Money! It is only a form of mathematics! In one way or another, every dollar we took was multiplied and returned, as we improved our machine and our understanding of the Transform and its power.

Q: To what end? To what gain?

A: Don't you understand? Don't you see how the transform field affected humanity? How it drew them in? How it gave them strength, and hope?

Q: And cocaine.

A: Bah! Cocaine! It is only a molecule! This drug did not cause the mass migration, surely you can see that. This rectum emanated positive wavelets of media-modulated N-space. That is what drew the people. It broadcast measurable particles of hope.

Q: Hype, you mean. Cocaine and hype.

A: Fool! Don't you see? The attention of the media merely created a substrate, a wave, onto which the Transform modulated its folding capacity, enveloping the earth. Do they not teach Orgone physics in this stupid country of yours?

Q: Tell me, Doctor, what were you trying to achieve on August 23rd, when you boosted power on your machine during the Concerts for Peace?

A: I was trying only to save human lives, and prevent suffering.

Q: Prevent suffering? You sucked a giant parking lot full of refugees and tanks into Agnes Cuddlebottom's rectum!

A: It was the N-space waves, they did that. I merely pressed the button.

Q: Ha! Didn't you realize the physiological effect of tasers on the rectal lining? Didn't you imagine?

A: Doctor Fokker is a gastroenterologist. I am a scientist. Nothing, up to that point, led us to believe that this operation could be dangerous in any way.

Q: Oh? Not dangerous? Not in any way?

A: Not ... at the time, no.

Q: Okay, super-genius: how about I stuff a tank up your ass, huh? And then you tell me if it feels dangerous!

A: Your outburst solves nothing. The past is the past. Not even the Spinejack Tranform can re-fold these tragic events.

Q: Madman!

A: If you must distribute blame, don't neglect to assign Mrs. Cuddlebottom her share.

Q: Agnes Cuddlebottom? For what? What did she do?

A: She woke up.

TRANSCRIPT FROM THE VOICE-RECORDER OF DR. FOKKER:

(Occasional low rumbling in the background.)

EF: Fokker here ... catching my breath ... I'm thanking
my astrology that I'm still pre-morbid, here on this steep slope
of the small intestine of Agnes Cuddlebottom, but I'm at a
loss to explain the situation in diagnostic terms. The entire
landscape has up-ended itself and is convulsing wildly. An
avalanche of cholesterol accretions detached from the side of
the colon and tumbled, taking myself and my captors along
with it. We skidded a long distance, we're all badly bruised,
shaken. McDermot, I'm afraid, is dead; he fell into a bile-filled
diverticulum and burst into flames. The remaining E. Coli
bacteria are surrounding me now, protecting me, they've dug
into the tissue below us with their cillia and intertwined with one
another, creating a kind of cocoon. I think they're just as scared
as I am. Our purchase is tentative on this slimy mucosa, and the
tremors continue. I'm clinging for my life to a greasy strand of
undigested fiber which I've secured to my fanny pack in case I
lose consciousness. I don't know how long I can last, hanging
here like this. The oxygen is tainted with an overpowering
stench of anaerobic decomposition. What is happening? Is
Mrs. Cuddlebottom being moved? Is she dying? Some kind of
ancillary operation must be underway, but what?
          (Distant loud rumble. Distant clicking, squeaking.)
          Did you hear that? Far below me, down in the yawning
pit of the intestine, I heard a loud, echoing screech! And now,

a distant roaring. And … I must be mistaken … no, something down there is emitting a pulsing red light … perhaps there's another endoscopic procedure underway? A rescue mission? Could it be? It's coming closer. It's very loud now, the roaring. I'm getting out my diagnostic binoculars.

No, it's not an endoscope, I see some type of … good lord!
(Roaring sound increases.)

Rising up from the depths … it's some species of worm! Some intestinal parasite! It's not a tapeworm but similar in length … it's brown … my God, it's macroscopic! It distends the intestine walls with its width! Its body is a dark, lumpy brown, flecked with irregularities. A crimson, laser-like wavelength of light glows within its anterior terminus, pulsing with a slow cardiac rhythm … It presents no normal head-like features except for teeth. Circular concentric rings of teeth, writhing, gnashing teeth … it's all teeth … I couldn't even make a guess at the genus of this thing, it's no parasite I've ever studied in all my years of gastro-enterology. But it's coming up … the sound is very unpleasant now, I'm having to yell over it … and the stench, the stench is triggering my gag reflex …

(Gagging.)

… and involuntary reverse peristalsis in my *eeeeEEEE-EEUGHH*

(Vomiting.)

Wait! The E. Coli bacteria are retreating! No! Please, take me with you! Come back! Wait! They're … dammit!

They've left me here! They're scuttling back up the intestinal wall! They've abandoned me! Bastards! Why did I trust them?

It's coming! The worm is coming for me! Oh God, it's getting closer!

Now, the intestine walls are rattling … they're going to clench again! Must … hang … on!

Q: You were Agnes Cuddlebottom's anaesthesiologist during the entirety of the Spinejack procedure, were you not?

Abel Hackman, Certified Registered Nurse Anaesthetist's Assistant:
Yeah, well, technically no. I was the CRNAA, which is the assistant to the CRNA, who takes responsibility. I just do the actual procedure, monitor the patient, the respirators, the vaporizers, the ... apparatuses, you know. The doodads.

Q: Who, then, was the CRNA in charge?

A: Doctor Fokker. He was in charge.

Q: But Doctor Fokker was inside the patient at that time. How did you communicate?

A: Oh right. No, actually, it was, um, the hospital has this rotating staff for that. The floor guy. He takes over when the overseeing guy is indisposed. But I never saw that guy. I know Doctor Spinejack talked to him just about every day though.

Q: It was you, then. Administering the drugs, adjusting dosages, and so on.

A: On the day shift, yeah, well ... you know, really I just mind the machine. The machine does the actual anaesthesiologizing.

141

Q: What machine?

A: The Lance! The Lance-Undertronic 8600, that's the anaesthesia system. It's brand new high-tech shit, it practically runs itself. It's bad-ass! There's just this screen with these five green lights, right? The five lights are inside little yellow boxes on the screen, and they wiggle around some, maybe this one's a little on the left, maybe that one bobs up and down, but as long as they stay inside those boxes? Then it's cool, the patient's happy, I'm doing nothing, and I'm getting paid! And even if a light goes out of a box and turns from green to, like, greenish yellow, right? Then a little dialog box comes up asking permission to fix the problem. Like, "Increase halothane PPM to 0.03?" or some shit. And you just click OK, and it does whatever thing, maybe you load a new cartridge of whatever drug, and the dots go back in the boxes and it's solid.

Or you can click Cancel, or Info ... but you wouldn't click Cancel, right? 'Cause something bad might happen. And we're supposed to never click Info, 'cause clicking Info crashed the machine once and some guy died.

Q: Where did you obtain your certification?

A: My ... huh?

Q: Your CRNAA. The C stands for "Certified," correct?

A: Oh, yeah, that's a good one. Actually, I'm not certified. The CRNA is certified, and I assist the CRNA, so that makes me the CRNAA, assistant to the CRNA or whoever is the anesthesiologist, or whatever. But I didn't take any special classes or anything. It's really not that hard. You just have to pay attention and watch the screen. And you know, sometimes change filters, refill bottles, rub K-Y on tubes and stuff, when it tells you to do that. They have classes on CRNA-ing at the school here, I was going to take some 'cause then they'd have to pay me more, but then the career guy in Facilities told me if I did that they'd have to replace me with somebody they could afford. And I love my job. So bag that!

Q: What anaesthesia did you use on Mrs. Cuddlebottom during her procedure?

A: Like, all of them. The Lance just kept switching it up. Every time that left-middle dot broke out of the top of its box, the Lance would beep and wig out and switch to another drug. It did halothane, isoflurane, sevoflurane, nitroflurane, xenon, thiopental, methohexital, diazepam, lorazepam, midazolam ... Ketamine ... hydromorphone ... xenon ... methaqualone, phencyclidine ... that's just the ones I can remember.

And I'm no doctor, right? But I've seen this sort of thing before with junkies. Their bodies are like: Drugs? Oh yeah! Gimme more! Let's rock! That lady was a serious user all her life, and I think she just got kind of generally immune to everything. So when she started to wake up, the machine would beep at me and I'd haul ass down to the dispensary to get whatever.

Q: How many times did she "wake up", as you say?

A: Maybe a dozen? Mostly early on. After a while we got her more under control. I hated that lady when she was awake.

Q: When you say "awake", do you mean she was—

A: Thrashing around yanking tubes, pulling off her mask, screaming. Lots of screaming, lots of swearing, calling everybody in the ward a whole bunch of names that I totally did not appreciate. She called me a pus-faced crackerjack! And she wanted us to stop the procedure, which, I mean, that's gotta be bad, right? We don't want that, do we?

Q: Was Mrs. Cuddlebottom able to move?

A: At first, yeah ... Doctor Spinejack had some guys come and slide in a restraint table under her, so we got her in restraints, so she didn't hurt herself. And at some point they fit her with like a gag thing ... well not a gag, they didn't gag her, it's more like ... it's like a medi-gag.

Q: A medi-gag?

A: Yeah, a health gag. It prevents her from biting her tongue, or letting her gums dry out. And you can still get gas into it, through a little pop-on valve on the side. But mostly it just shuts her up! Which frankly ... like I say, I love my job, but I don't see why I have to listen to that shit while I'm trying to help save a person!

Like for instance: if I was a fireman, right? And I walked into some burning building to do rescues, and the building had a voice, and the building was all, "fuck you dude! I'm all on fire and shit! Let me burn, you pus-face crackerjack bitch!" ... then I'm like, why should I hose you down? Why should I pull cats out of your sketchy basement? When you're such a total dick-wad? You know? Did I light you on fire? Y'know?

Q: Totally.

A: Same with that lady. All she ever said was "cracker" and "devil" and "eat a dick!" and "let me go!" and "get this submarine outta my ass!" And she'd pray, a lot. She was a very religious lady. Even with the gag on, I could tell sometimes she was praying.

Q: Tell me about the events on the last day.

A: Wow, let's see ... well ... you know, I was hanging out by the machine I guess, texting my g-friend—she's all like, "SUP?" and I'm all like, "BORD!"—everything was fine, casual, but then all of a sudden the Lance beeps at me, and, like, suddenly three of the dots are outside of the boxes, and the middle left one is all red and bouncing against the top of the screen. Just like that! And Agnes turns her head and looks right at me, and her eyes are wide open, all red and glowing. I'm freaking out, and the Lance says "Analgesic failure—switch to diacetylmorphine?" and I click "OK!", and it says "Insert diacetylmorphine cartridge in the flashing bin."

So I run to the dispensary—did I mention it's on the total opposite end of the wing?—and at the dispensary I slide my card and type in the code for diacetylmorphine, and the dispensary says: "CRNAA Not Authorized—Refer to CRNA." Then I run Dr. Spinejack's card, and it says the exact same thing. 'Cause I guess diacetylmorphine is some kind of fancy shit that people steal. I run a couple more cards, just ones that doctors left lying around that I sort of found and picked up, but no dice. Not Authorized.

Fuck, I say.

So I run back up the wing, I stop at every nurse's station to try to find that guy who's the floor anesthesiologist, 'cause he's got to have the right card. And I find the guy, right outside the post-hernia Pilates lounge, sipping a latte and trimming his nails, and I'm screaming at him: Dude! Gimme your card! I need diacetylmorphine, stat! And he folds his arms, looks down his nose at me like I'm some skanky drug addict, but I tell him: Dude! I'm the CRNAA and it's an emergency, stat! And he says "What patient?" And I'm like "Room 101!" and he's like "Oh, right, her ..." He knows. He totally knows. But still, he says he has to see her before he can prescribe diacetylmorphine!

I'll tell you, that guy was a to-tal douche! Nurse Tuttle. Nurse Glen "I-Am-A-Douche" Tuttle, R.N., CRNA, Douche. You should interrogate that guy, not me.

But we go into Room 101—and Agnes is, like, trying to sit up in bed! Even though we've got her wrists clamped in these Medi-Clamp Wrist Systems! She's shaking her head, twisting and shit, bad scene. And moaning. And her eyes, man ... it's like she swallowed some laser pointers or something.

So Nurse Douchebag goes up to the Lance, which is still saying "Insert diacetylmorphine cartridge in the flashing bin," and the bin is still flashing, but then? What does he do, Certified Nurse Douchebag?

He clicks Cancel! Like this woman's life is just a game to him!

And I'm just standing there watching ... 'cause I guess I trust him, 'cause I guess he's the floor guy, the CRNA, even though Dr. Spinejack was really specific that he didn't want the floor CRNA anywhere near my station. But I don't know what else to do. What else could I do?

The Lance is back to saying: "Analgesic failure—switch to diacetylmorphine?" So what does the CRNA do? Does he click OK! and let me go get the fucking diacetylmorphine? No.

Does he click Cancel! and then, like, apply some special CRNA kung-fu medical knowledge of his own to solve the problem? No.

He clicks Info.

That douche!

And yeah! The Lance-Undertronic 8600 machine totally reboots. It goes BONGGG! and the screen goes black, and then it says "Starting Windows," and then it just sits there, spinning the little spinner ... while all of the pumps and beepers and everything go quiet. And the Medi-Clamp Wrist Systems and Ankle Systems just go pop, pop, pop, pop! Emergency release.

Nurse Tuttle looks at me, I look at him ... we look at Agnes ... and that lady has bloody red murder pouring out of her eyes ...

ARCHIVAL TRANSCRIPT PROVIDED BY WPMS-23 NEWS ARCHIVES: BRENDA SPONGE REPORTING.

BS: Colonic catastrophe! Anal massacre! Vietnam in the hiney! These are just a few of the words being used here, in the transverse colon of Agnes Cuddlebottom, to describe the overwhelming crisis taking place all around us. I'm Brenda Sponge, and this is Operation Cuddlebottom: The Quickening.

I'm speaking to you from a makeshift refugee center on the far side of Lake Mucosa. Across the lake you can see the Grindstone Center for Peace, site of the Agnes Cuddlebottom Festival for Peace, where twenty thousand National Guard peace-keepers are still struggling to subdue hundreds of thousands of unruly peace protesters, using guns, tear gas and, it has been reported, grenades. Several hundred adult-contemporary music fans have died in the conflict already.

Yet despite the violence and regular interruptions in power, the Concerts for Peace lurch bravely onward. The organizers of the event have issued a statement promising amnesty for all protesters and gatecrashers, plus additional encores from last night's headlining band Cutesnake, who played a disappointing 15-minute set, plus an unspecified number of "positive vibes", if the audience will lay down their weapons and, quote, "take a chill pill." Unfortunately, no such pills are being distributed at this time, although many audience members were caught on camera freebasing cocaine.

Here on the north side of Lake Mucosa, the situation is relatively calm. Workers from Mount Venuda Search & Rescue have erected a temporary processing facility, surrounded by chain link safety fence and barbed safety wire. They are encouraging the traumatized soaking-wet refugees to wait inside for eventual assistance. But the traumatized concertgoers keep coming; some in motorboats, some paddling rafts made from lawn chairs and coolers, others collapsing in exhaustion on the shore, having swam the entire breadth of the lake. It's a long swim, and there are unconfirmed reports of bloody drowned bodies bobbing on the surface of the lake like so many feces in a—what?

(Loud rumbling, shaking, screams.)

My god! It's an earthquake! And the lake! It's rising up, its ...

(Screams. Huge waves breaking.)

Tsunami-force waves are crashing against the shore! Slapping aside the fences! Washing the refugees backwards towards the precipice of the ascending colon! My God, it's horrible!

(Screams. Deep roaring and hissing.)

Look! Like Old Faithful, a huge geyser of steam is rising up from the cecum! What could this mean? Hang on! Oh my—the smell! It's just awful!

(Screams. Louder rumbling. Larger waves.)

Look! A massive brown form is rising up from the precipice—good Jimminy Christmas! Sam, are you getting this? A gigantic, tooth-faced demonic brown snake of some kind is slithering up out of the ascending colon! Filling the air with its awful stench!

What does this mean? What does this strange being want from us? Is it friend or foe?

This just in: it's foe! That's confirmed! It's eating some refugees now, in an unmistakable foe-like manner, licking them up off the ground with a long, thin silver tongue and then, chewing them up ... chewing up the people ... the refugees are waving lighters and cell phones at the creature, to no effect ... folks, this is a KPMS exclusive! But here comes another big wave—

(Continued screams. Giant wave crashing. Chopper blades.)
A new development! Above us now you can hear the roar of the Mount Venuda Search & Rescue Heli-Vac Unit! It's flying toward the monster! It's blasting a deafening strain of gangsta rap from its public address system! It looks like MVS&R are spoiling for a fight!

They're launching air-to-air missiles at the creature! Go Jock! You show that thing .... you just ... are you getting this Sam? The missiles bounced off, but they're trying again, they're going into ... negative, here's an update: MVS&R are not attacking the creature! Rather, they too are being eaten! And this is live! The entire helicopter is disappearing, sorry, has disappeared down the throat of this vast, strange, foul-smelling foe. And it's still coming ... still coming ... the odor is overwhelming ... it's coming closer, it's coming straight at us ...

This is a Brenda Sponge KPMS exclusive: I'm going to die now! Sam, be sure to get this! It's—whoops!

(Severe rumbling and tumbling. Non-stop screams. Giant thud. Slithering.)
Sam? Wake up! Wake up and point that thing at me! Sam! Hello? Is this rolling? Brenda Sponge here, KPMS ... this creature, this fearsome, deadly, and absolutely nasty-smelling thing, has spared us. It's passing by now, scraping past us like a giant mudslide, its long, tapered, lumpy girth sliding into the depths of Lake Mucosa, its demonic thirst for blood apparently sated, for now ... apparently uninterested in consuming a veteran news reporter of fifteen years, apparently that's not good enough for this evil monster ... probably it just doesn't consider me important, probably it only eats men, that would be typical for such a fiendish snake. But this is not over yet! We're giving chase ... Sam?

Sam! *(Expletive)* Sam, wake up! Will you get your ass off the ground and stop bleeding? I can't hold this stupid camera and still probe the news! *(Expletive)* butt-snake, I'll show that thing. Fine! Just give me the camera! Come on, let go of it! Let! Go! If you're asleep why are you so damn stiff? We're losing the story! Look, it's getting away, there's nothing left but—wait!

What's this? Folks, it appears someone is straddling this disgusting stink-monster's tail! Riding on its back like it's some kind of elephant! They're coming closer, it looks like two people, one adult and one child ... or possibly not a child, but—but— oh!—could it be?

Oh! My! Jesus *(expletive)* *(expletive)* Christ on a *(expletive)* pogo stick!

It's Jojo! Jojo the Monkey! With Doctor Fokker!

Q:　　Do you have an actual name? Or should I just call you "Butt-Snake?"

A:　　BEHOLD NIDHOGG! THE DREAD BITER! FLESH-EATER OF THE SINISTER LORD! "BUTT-SNAKE" IS ALSO ACCEPTABLE—AS LONG AS YOU TREMBLE WHEN YOU SAY IT!

Q:　　Yes sir! But ... how did you end up in Agnes Cuddlebottom's intestines?

A:　　I WAS SUMMONED!

Q:　　Summoned how? By whom?

A:　　SUMMONED BY DARK WORSHIP! TO CONSUME THE FILTHY SOULS OF THE EXPLOTERS!

Q:　　The exploiters? Oh ... right! Those guys! Well, I haven't seen them around here, but I'll certainly—

A:　　BEHOLD THE WRATH OF NIDHOGG!

(Screams of unholy terror. Roaring, crashing, general panic. Sounds of human bodies torn asunder. Chewing, slurping, writhing.)

Q:　　Ouch ... um ... okay ... how many souls was that?

A:　　SEVEN HUNDRED PUNY SOULS!

(Massive unholy burping.)

Q: Oh God, oh God, oh God ... okay, Mr. Maktub, does that mean you're, um, leaving now? Your work is done here, right?

A: PUNY FLESHLING! STILL I HUNGER! YOUR GOD HAS FORSAKEN YOU! ALL YOUR SOULS SHALL BE CONSUMED! ALL SHALL TWIST AND BURN, IMPALED IN THE PIT OF THE DAMNED!

Q: Wait, but ... all our souls? *My* soul? What did I do? I'm the good guy! You can't just eat my soul!

A: SILENCE, SNIVELLER! I SHALL RETURN TO BRUNCH UPON YOUR ENTRAILS!

(Splashing, gurgling ... deep sighing ... weeping ...)

Q: Nice job, Doctor Spinejack. If you even are a doctor.

DR. OTTO SPINEJACK:
     My Ph.D. in subatomic physics is unquestionable. But thank you.

Q: Shut up! Tell me what happened to the Spinejack Transform Field when Agnes Cuddlebottom freed herself!

A: Our machine, of course, has multiple fail-safe systems to protect both patient and operator in any unexpected event, even one as potentially catastrophic as sudden anal disconnect. These systems worked flawlessly. There was no danger. Had Mrs. Cuddlebottom simply allowed our staff to return her to bed, and to reconnect the machine before an inevitable N-space field collapse, we could have minimized the tragedy.
     But that woman! What strength! What anger! A she-devil from Hell! Three men together could not subdue her! She tossed us aside like little boys in the path of a wild boar! And the way she screamed, as she ran down the hall ... she was quite uncooperative, I am saying.

Q: What do you mean, "inevitable N-space field collapse"?

A: Oh, please understand, we can sustain the Impedance Transform Intersection indefinitely! Our machine is built with two of each component. Even when it breaks it continues to function. And even a momentary impedance mismatch is not harmless, because the colon, it resonates systemically with this energy. The transform is a note, played on a violin string that we scrape with an N-dimensional bow. It decays quite slowly, this note that we play on this violin. It is a pleasant, beautiful sound. And quite safe.

Q: Safe?

A: When used properly, yes. Completely safe.

Q: Doctor Spinejack .... are you blind? Have you lost all reason? Look around you!

A: My answer to all of this is of course No. You simply do not understand—

Q: Shut up, Spinejack! Look! Behold, your pleasant and beautiful sound! Here we are, as far as we know. the last surviving humans on what remains of Earth! Floating together on this evil repugnant barge of ... of giant feces! Feces, Otto! Shit and Ski-Doos, lashed together with microphone cables! With nothing to sustain us but cocaine, roast monkey meat, and, yes, feces!

A: You are wrong! I never intended this. I simply—

Q: Shut up! We are floating, Otto, as you know, in a sea of shit! A sea of pure human diarrhea! As sick and horrible a hell as any one of us could imagine! Some have died from the smell alone! And soon, Otto, that demonic shit-snake will surface again, and chew up some more of us in its blender of a face, until we are all finally dipped in shit and dead! That is the end of the world your miracle has given us, Doctor Spinejack! We're all dead! Open your eyes!

A: No, no, no! Don't you see?

Q: The only thing you have left to give us, Otto, before we throw you to the snake, is answers. Did you truly not foresee these tragic events? At all? The destruction of the earth? The doom of humanity, of all life? Answer me!

A: Humanity is not doomed. There is a survivor!

Q: Who? Who survived?

A: Agnes Cuddlebottom! She lives on!

Q: Agnes? Agnes exploded! The contents of her bowels amplified to infinite size!

A: Ha, ha, ha! You are no physicist! Let me explain ... when Agnes Cuddlebottom stole out into the hospital hallway and ran to the toilet, the tragic contents of her intestines had not yet begun to unfold. She only knew of an urgency in her lower torso ... it had been some weeks since she had moved her bowels. And, upon reaching her goal, she pushed forth her lower diaphragm, clutching her bowels in such a way that the N-space resonance ringing within her was tightened, raising in pitch and strength. This, in turn, began the inevitable—sorry, I should say the tragically *avoidable* self-re-amplification of the Field, and everything within it. The space-time fabric of the universe began then to curl up around her rectal region even as it unfolded elsewhere—the well-known Krophnitz Preservation Of Folding Conjecture, you recall —wrapping around her body, trapping her in an N-dimensional bubble, even as the waves elongated and uncurled their complexities across the earth.

     And so, in a classic space-time topographic transform, the universe within Agnes Cuddlebottom and the universe outside exchanged their coordinates across a vertex drawn along the imaginary N-space asymptote! If chalk had five dimensions,

I could draw you a simple diagram that would—

Q: You are so full of shit.

A: Ha! To employ such metaphor in this place is tactless. What you must believe is this: I did not kill Agnes Cuddlebottom. She lives on!

Q: Where? Where is she?

A: Outside us, outside all of us. Now, she is the universe! Now, she envelops all that we know! She is God, now, looking down upon us. And I know that she forgives us. If we pray to her, she will save us!

Q: Save us? How? How can she save us?

A: Get on your knees! Pray to her! Pray to Agnes! Beg her forgiveness! Beg her help!

(Bowing, scraping. Moaning.)

Q: Stop that! You, all of you! Stop! Doctor Spinejack, you are mad! Insane!

A: Unbeliever! Open your heart! Agnes, show him your love! Reveal yourself!

OTHERS: Unbeliever!

(Bowing, scraping, prayer, uulation. Throwing of feces.)

Q: You're all on crack! And if even for a moment I did believe that Agnes Cuddlebottom were God—

A: Agnes! Reveal yourself!

OTHERS: Reveal yourself!

Q: If Agnes is God, then I expect lightning bolts to strike us all down right now! To strike you all down for what you've done! And me as well, for how I failed—

(Immense sound of rushing water.)

Q: Look! On the horizon! A whirlpool! Growing larger!

A: It's Agnes! She's saving us! Rescuing us from this universe!

Q: It's too close! Everybody! We have to paddle away from it! Paddle now! It's our only hope! Come on, everybody! Reach over the edge of the raft ... and just, you know ... stick your legs down in that ... eww ...

(Conspicuous silence.)

A: Agnes will save us. Agnes forgives all!

Q: I wish I believed you.

OTHERS: Agnes! Agnes save us! We're coming! We're sorry! We love you!

(A huge swirling of feces.
An immense rushing of water.
A giant sucking sound.
The jiggling of God's handle.
Silence.)

157

CRAZY SHITTING PLANET

For Kevin

THE FAT PEOPLE

The fat people are hundreds of feet tall, clad in the finest exoskeletal fashions, giant zeppelins of money and power and fat. They block out the sun with their immensity, staring down at us from the heavens with their pale, simple, hungry faces, their compound eyes as big as soccer balls, their bulbous bellies vast as astrodomes. Usually they eat us, though occasionally they toy with us, strafing us with food or clean water or scraps of the past. Either way, they own us. The fat people own everything: the air, the water, the sky; words, speech, thought; the past, the future. All of these things belong to the fat people now, while we little creatures on the ground are left to scavenge in their shit for crumbs and scurry to evade the punishment of their mighty crushing feet.

Call me Cheeseburger. I have no family; my mother died from the general sickness long ago, the same disease of everything that gives me this cough, cough, cough. My father was eaten by a fat person, almost a year ago. A particularly obese, giggling pale sky-bag that swooped down on us one day as Father and Son foraged for edible plastic in one of the many massive piles of shit and debris which rain down from the bloody orange sky. I had just discovered, half buried in stinking fat-person feces, a beautiful antique laptop computer from the late Stuff Era. Praising our luck, we had begun to dine together on the tiny morsels of keyboard, when the sky went dark. Silent and deadly, the fat woman smiled down at us, the bulbous folds of her face pinched into a tent-like mask of hungry anticipation. There was nowhere to hide.

To save my life, Father shoved me into the feces, rendering me grody and unpalatable. As I scraped the stinking brown paste from my eyes I watched an immense pink hand, encrusted with stunningly huge jeweled baubles and two massive Rolex replicas, plunge down and scoop up my father, who struggled not a twitch. He only cried out "Eat or be eaten, kiddo!" as he slowly ascended out of earshot, towards the hideous bloated jowls of the levitating obesity. It studied him for a moment, sniffing him with its massive, surgically enhanced nose, and then with incredible vicious speed it gobbled him up.

Inside the fat person, I knew, lasers and grinders and robotic viscera flayed Father alive, stripping him skin to bone, boiling him down to nutrition and energy, and injecting his jellied existence directly down the gullet of the rich bastard at its core. Satisfied, the fat person emitted a jet of flaming methane from its rectal thrusters and shot back up into the sky, to the place where the fat people float forever.

And then I was alone in the world. Except for my friend Aimless.

My friend Aimless found a telescope, and now makes a study of the fat people. Gazing through his telescope at the floating city of fat, he says, is a quiet way to pass the time. They have built Fat Heaven up there, he tells me. In their titanic city of pearl and silver, held aloft by the constant effort of nuclear reactors, the fat people dance and sing, hold beauty contests, stage immense operas, copulate on clouds, stuff giant bales of money adoringly in one another's asses, and endlessly elaborate upon their total consumption of everything. They fling their refuse down to earth, where we tiny things that remain crawl out of our holes and race to feed upon it, while low-flying fat people make cruel sport of us.

I hate them. But Aimless watches them and only laughs.

The fat people are strong, they are smart, they have every good thing that ever was, all of it. All the earth's bounty is tightly concentrated in their gargantuan fists. They do not share. They don't have to. The great struggle is over and the fat people have won. I used to dream of a day when they would eat the last rock of the earth and find themselves, at last, hungry and unfed. But Aimless has watched them soar away into space, perhaps searching for other planets, other universes to eat and shit upon and throw away. The fat people want to eat the sun, and when they've run out of sun I'm sure their hunger will lead them on to other stars. They'll never have enough.

GERTIE THE WHALE

Aimless says he's in love with a whale. He says the whale comes to him in his dreams, singing to him when he's sleeping. He says the whale has beautiful eyes. He says the whale's name is Gertie, and he wants to find her something for her birthday. Aimless tells me all this as we pick through a layer of potato chip bags, used diapers and syringes with our digging sticks. I'm looking for something we can eat, smoke, or feed to Mrs. Teeth. Aimless is looking for a present for his whale.

A thing about Aimless: he loves animals. And loving something that is dead and gone can be hard. I try not to think about my family; sometimes in my dreams I see my Father's face rising into the sky, and I'm overcome with anger, I shake with rage, I weep. But Aimless is always excited to tell me about rats he almost saw, or insects he found traces of, or bones he dug up which might not have died too long ago. He's ever hopeful.

There are no more animals, I try to explain. We ate them all. The fat people ate all the tasty ones and the starving people ate the rest a long, long time ago. Every now and then someone might discover a dead animal in the general piles of trash and shit that we dig through, but those animals are ages dead, mummified by trash. And if we do ever find such a dead, rotten, disgusting animal, we have to feed it to Mrs. Teeth.

There are no more animals, but there are lots of drugs. Drugs are one of the things the fat people happily shit on us. Six months ago it rained feces and marijuana for two days. Everyone in our colony smoked and smoked and smoked it, adults and children both, until our brains ran out our ears. Then, while we lay passed out in a happy blue haze of shit-stinking bliss, the fat people came down and ate dozens of us. That's how stupid we are.

Aimless lives in a rusting automobile, I think it was once a Dodge Caravan, that is lodged in the side of a cliff of scrap metal just above the reeking, reeling tide of the shit-dark ocean, overlooking a beach of slime. Nobody ever comes here because the smell is so terrible. This is where Aimless lives alone, and hoards his treasure, and smokes the leftover marijuana and dried feces.

Aimless is very rich. All of us dig through the rotten trash to survive—what else is there to do?—but Aimless is luckier than the rest. Aimless finds incredible things, constantly. He has magic powers. He has The Knack. And while most people throw back what they can't eat or smoke or burn for fuel, Aimless is a collector.

Aimless collects animals. He has hundreds of metal fish, several rubber snakes, a stuffed bird with no head, and numerous porcelain cats, or parts of porcelain cats, or broken shards of porcelain which he says remind him of cats. All of these decorate his tight, frozen, stinking metal home, or are hoarded in the catacombs of scrap underneath.

Aimless collects photographs. Pictures from the times before the fat overlords owned absolutely everything, the times when stupid people like us still had clothing and lived indoors and ate food. Most photographs from the Stuff Era are curiously inedible, but I would still gladly burn them for heat. Aimless, however, would rather sleep in the cold than sacrifice these scraps of paper.

Aimless collects nautical supplies. He has an anchor, and some rope. He has glass floats and old, rotten nets, useful for catching the fish that used to live in the sea, but no longer. He has an eye patch—I'm not sure what makes this a nautical supply, but he insists it's crucial. He has a rusty compass and a pile of mildewed nautical charts. He once caught me chewing on one of them—mildew is considered a delicacy in our colony—and smashed me in the nose with the anchor.

"Without those charts," he said, "how can I find Gertie?"

Aimless collects so many things ... anything bright and shiny, anything ancient and hand-worn, anything that might be at home in his dreams. Anything and everything useless and inedible, he caches and catalogues in the holes he's dug beneath his van in the side of his cliff, all of his lovely collections waiting to be someday dragged down into the shit-dark sea by a tidal wave of crap.

Aimless is insane. But he's also rich, and he has a lot of drugs. I'm happy that he calls me his friend. Sometimes he vanishes for months at a time, but when he's around, we dig in the trash together. I watch the sky with his telescope, ready to dive for cover if the fat people notice us, while Aimless waves a crooked stick back and forth over the shit-greased piles of debris, his eyes closed, listening, wandering in short steps, sniffing the fetid air ... and then suddenly he dives, attacking the earth with his digging stick, scraping and scuttling at the plastic bags and debris with silent assurance until he conjures forth some beautiful or meaningful or edible fragment from the Age of Stuff.

This time, it's a small plastic model of some kind of boat. He holds it triumphantly up to the sky, smiling with pride. A toy. A yellow submarine.

I ask him the ultimate question of my people: are you going to eat that? But I know better. What he has found is clearly a nautical supply. So we keep digging, searching for the perfect gift for an imaginary whale.

ARE YOU GOING TO EAT THAT?

Rubber is chewy. I can chew on a piece of rubber for days before it loses its flavor and finally begins to crumble. One of my favorite things to chew is an old shoe, especially if it carries the flavor of an antique human foot.

Plastic is crunchy. There are many kinds of plastic; some kinds I can eat, others make me vomit. But they all provide texture. Because I am always coughing, I must eat very slowly. It's easy to choke on plastic.

Shit tastes terrible. But it's all over everything. The turds of the flying fat people are the only steady component of our diets. We scrape, we rub, we tap and polish everything we pull out of the shit-soaked ground, but still, we eat an awful lot of shit.

Every now and then, the fat people throw us a bone. It amuses them to do so. The day I was born, it rained shit-covered cheeseburgers. They shot down from the sky in hot greasy fusillades, smacking people in the heads and backs, exploding on the ground. I'm told it was the most beautiful day in our history, a day without hunger, a day my father loved to remember. That's why he named me Cheeseburger.

Or else he planned to eat me.

THE WEATHER

Today it rained shit and exercise videos. These were shit-coated cardboard boxes painted, on the front, with a picture of an incredibly clean, well-fed woman, a woman with all her teeth and perfect skin, clad in angelic blue and grey clothing, standing in a warm, sun-filled room, smiling, smiling, smiling. And on the back of each box, her solemn promise: you will lose the weight you want to lose. And keep it off.

Inside each box was a black plastic tray, and centered on each tray was a shiny, reflective disc. I find these discs in the trash piles all the time. They are difficult to eat. But the cardboard box itself wasn't bad. The ink tastes terrible, but the boxes were flat with a smooth surface; you could scrape just about all the shit off of them.

One month ago, it rained shit and George Foreman Grills. Giant useless iron apparatuses from the era of propane gas in canisters. One of these grills fell on my cousin Beef and killed him. Then Mrs. Teeth ate his body. Many of the other grills exploded into bits of jagged metal when they hit the ground, scattering razor-edged shards that still cut my feet when I step on them. My aunt Crazins stepped on one, and her foot became infected. Her leg turned fat and yellow, and she was unable to run. So Mrs. Teeth ate her too.

One thing about the weather: if you don't like it, stick around and it'll get worse. Sometimes it rains Sony PlayStation Twos and shit. Sometimes it rains flat plasma televisions and shit.

I remember the horrible day when it rained NordicTrack Fitness Systems and shit. Many people died.

MRS. TEETH

The woman in our colony called Mrs. Teeth is much bigger than the rest of us, and older. She's not fat or huge like the people in the sky, but compared to my own gaunt stick-frame of a body she is like a great pillar of angry meat with huge, loose, hairy breasts and long, snatching fingers. She is very very clean and white, because she refuses to eat shit.

Mrs. Teeth doesn't suffer from the general sickness. She doesn't cough, she isn't racked with chills or pox on her skin. She is tall and wide and healthy. She has all her teeth, and she likes to bare them. "Grrrrrr!" she says. Her eyes are close together and her voice is loud and frightening.

Because Mrs. Teeth doesn't have the sickness, there isn't much she can eat. The fungus in my belly, I've learned, can break down almost anything and convert it into fuel for The Host. That's me—I am The Host. The fungus in my belly is slowly eating me, very slowly it is eating us all, but it also helps us to survive on this landscape of trash and shit. The point of my survival is lost on me, but feeding the hunger is a habit I can't break. The fungus in my belly is like a starving child, always crying. I like to think that it loves me, my hungry sickness. I try to be a good host.

Mrs. Teeth is a poor host. Her fungus left her.

Mrs. Teeth is family. She's my mother's sister's husband's mother's sister. Since my father's sister's husband was also her half-brother, Mrs. Teeth is also my aunt. We are all family in this colony. That's why my lower lip curls around toward my left ear, and also why my cousin Beef had no arms to deflect the George Foreman Grill that crushed him. We are defective recycled products.

But we're family, so we look after each other. Whenever one of us finds something in the trash that Mrs. Teeth could eat, they set it aside for her, even though we too are starving. We do this for her out of love.

We also do it so she won't eat us. Mrs. Teeth is so strong, so fast, so hungry. When one of our colony dies, or is about to die, or shows signs of possibly nearing death, Mrs. Teeth smiles, and begins to drool.

Mrs. Teeth is a very pious woman. She worships the fat people in the sky, the gods of Fat Heaven. She believes our fat owners are the source of all goodness, wisdom and justice—not that we have any of that down here. But you must never argue with Mrs. Teeth, because she bites, and her teeth are full of diseases that stick in your flesh and make you sick. Then, when you grow ill, Mrs. Teeth follows you around waiting for you to fall.

Mrs. Teeth becomes very angry if anyone ever complains about the precious gifts the fat people have shat upon us. "Rejoice!" she cries whenever it comes dumping down. "Hallelujah!" she screams, and dances, and points at the sky. "Praise them!" And if you are near her when this happens, then you had better bow down and pray, because, as I said before, she bites.

Mrs. Teeth is very insane, very dangerous. I try very hard to stay away from her. But I would rather be eaten by Mrs. Teeth than give anything, even thanks, to those evil fat pigs in the sky.

AIMLESS'S GUITAR

Last night it was too cold to sleep, so I went to find Aimless and his drugs. I found him on the edge of the cliff, sitting cross-legged on a dry patch of elevated sky-turd ... and do you know what I found him doing?

I found him playing a guitar!

He found it in the trash, he said. An entire guitar! I have never even found a box the size of a guitar, and if I had found such a box it would have been crushed and full of feces.

Aimless's guitar is clean, uncrushed, it has three intact strings and spaces for three more. Maybe Aimless will find those too, the lucky bastard.

Oh, how my stomach churned, gazing at that beautiful, beautiful guitar. I have never even found a stick as thick as the neck of that guitar, in all my years of trash. Oh, how I dreamed of seizing it from him and lighting it afire, just to bring a moment's warmth to my cold, naked life. How I longed to bite off a corner of that guitar—just a tiny corner—and feel the splintery wood dissolving in my stomach.

Aimless strummed the guitar tunelessly, gazing out into the freezing, shit-dark sea. He ignored my astonishment over his sudden production of this astounding relic, and my anger at the useless way he toyed with it—as if he and I and all of us in the colony were not tumbling down a long slope of hunger and desperation. As if trees still existed, and guitars grew on them. Madman!

In my mind's eye, I killed Aimless right there, and I ate him. Aimless is even smaller and scrawnier than me, and oblivious to danger. I could kill him with my bare hands. In my mind I built a fire of his guitar, and roasted his flesh over it, and ate him. And I was warm and full and happy and alone, in my mind's eye.

But I couldn't really do that to my only friend.

Aimless ignored me. He just strummed the guitar, and sang a song to his girlfriend:

> *Gertie, baby sweetie,*
> *Meet me by the shore,*
> *Where nobody is wailin'*
> *On the whales no more.*
>
> *Open up your ocean,*
> *Lead me to your deep,*
> *Lay me in the cradle*
> *Where the baby whales sleep.*
>
> *We will swim into the sun,*
> *We will dive into the sky,*
> *We will float along the river*
> *And we're never gonna die.*
>
> *I will hold you in my arms,*
> *I will love you 'till I'm sore,*
> *Oh Gertie, baby sweetie,*
> *If you meet me by the shore.*

"How are you going to hold a whale in your arms?" I had to ask.

Then Aimless stopped playing his guitar. He gazed at me, annoyed.

"Are you saying Gertie is fat?" he asked.

"Well, she's a whale, isn't she?"

He made no reply, except to return to strumming his guitar. It was clear he wasn't going to eat that.

Eventually he said: "Yes, she's a whale. But she's special!"

Later we smoked some drugs and Aimless fell asleep on the cold cliffside. I was hungry, shuddering, confused and angry. And there lay Aimless's guitar next to him, begging me to take it.

Love makes no sense to me. You can't eat it, you can't smoke it, you can't burn it for fuel. I feel the dull warmth of my family ties, but family ties are provisional. Family is a courtesy that everyone extends because everyone so desperately needs the favor returned. When it's time to feed Mrs. Teeth, family love weighs as much in one hand as one edible plastic door handle weighs in the other. Love is flimsy and disposable. It may be worth something, but not much.

I could never, ever fall in love with an imaginary whale.

But neither could I eat my friend's guitar.

EXTREMELY BAD NEWS

I am doomed!

I always wondered how long I had to live, and now I know. I am definitely going to die, I can see it all coming now.

This morning I heard the news from my cousin Earwax, as we worked the trash pile together. He laughed when he told me, and poked me in my cough-wracked chest with his trash stick:

Mrs. Teeth has fallen in love with me!

Me!

Earwax laughed and laughed, until he folded over in a fit of wheezing. And then I spied Mrs. Teeth, far off over the bluff of trash. Just her huge head poked above the horizon, watching us, peering at me with her close-together eyes, and I knew this was no joke. Even at that distance I could see the passion burning in her like infection.

Why me? How did her mind settle on me? She ate her previous husband less than a month ago. How can she need another one so soon?

It's only a matter of time now. I am doomed, doomed, doomed! I need to hide. I need to escape.

Ever since this morning she has been following me! She keeps her distance, for now, but I know she'll be coming closer.

Probably she is carrying a present for me, probably some disgusting bouquet of my relatives' bones. When she catches me she will blush, and then bashfully hand me these bony flowers, the fingers and toes of my cousins and uncles.

She will ask me if I like this, and if I tell the truth she will kill me.

She will ask me to hold her hand, and if I refuse, she will eat me.

That horrible madwoman will clutch my head with her huge grasping fingers and pull it towards her own, and ask me to kiss her on her diseased, toothy mouth! If I refuse, she'll bite out my tongue! That is what love means to Mrs. Teeth!

And on top of all that, other bad news: a storm is brewing in Fat Heaven. That's what Aimless told me when I went to visit him. He has been studying them through his telescope, and he says they're angry. Some fat person has offended some other fat person, and they are all up there taking sides, getting ready to fight. Aimless says it has something to do with a spoiled romance.

This has happened before. The last time the fat people pummeled each other in the sky above us, they oozed blood and shit and vomit and useless consumer products for days and days. My cousin Snackables was swept up in the putrid gore and washed away to drown in the shit-dark sea, it fell so thick and slippery. Even our trash was contaminated with their bile and their blood. We had to dig for weeks to reach some relatively clean garbage. All because two floating fat men had to prove their relative worth to some floating fat woman in the sky.

Love! If the word Love had a head, I would stab it in the eye with my stick.

It's so bad, this news, I can't even think. I can only sit on the cliff next to Aimless, clutch my head, and listen to him babble while he plays his guitar.

Aimless says that there's nothing to worry about. Aimless says everything will be fine, because Aimless is building a submarine. As soon as this submarine is ready, he says, the two of us can sail away into the shit-dark sea, thence to meet up with his whale girlfriend. "I think she has a sister," he tells me, winking, while he strums the notes.

Aimless is insane, but I appreciate his willingness to help. I sit there beside him on the cliff, and listen to him sing his song to his whale, and for a moment I forget to worry. Foolish me.

Did you know that people in love are drawn to music? Yes, music attracts lovers like shit once attracted flies, before we ate all the flies.

Music now attracts Mrs. Teeth. Here she comes, shambling across the trash-mound toward us, shoving through the twisted scrap. I could run, but she would catch me. I could hide, but she would tear Aimless's home apart looking for me, scatter his collections, sink his submarine. So I sink deep inside myself, perched there on the cliff, hiding inside my own skin, waiting for the horror.

I never knew love could feel like this.

Mrs. Teeth tramples up behind us. "Such beautiful music!" she barks, clapping her hands in glee. Before either of us can react, she has grabbed Aimless's guitar out of his hands and is shaking it upside-down, trying to dump the music out of the hole so she can eat it. Aimless grabs at the guitar and she slaps him to the ground with one meaty hand. She shakes it and shakes it, a dumb confused look on her face, but no edible musicians fall out of the guitar. Then, she holds it out to me.

"It's a present," she says. "I like you. Take it!"

I take it, and hand it back to Aimless.

"Now we're friends!" she giggles. "Do you like that?"

I know it's important to lie when answering this question, but I just don't think I can do it. Honesty is my handicap. Honesty and my harelip. I want to say nothing, but I know Mrs. Teeth will reach down my throat with her ravaging hands and pull the truth up out of my belly if I don't speak it.

"It's a nice guitar," I offer.

She reaches between my legs and grabs my genitals in one

cold, clutching hand!

"Wanna be my boyfriend?" she asks, grinning. With her other hand she raises a hairy breast toward my face. A drop of saliva runs from the corner of her stinking mouth.

"Be my boyfriend and fuck me? Wanna?" she asks, leering.

I really don't want to answer this question! But she leans over me, pushing her idiot lips at mine, squeezing me painfully. I go cross-eyed just looking into the beady eyes in her pinched-together face.

Just then, two things happen for which I will always be grateful.

First, there is a loud cracking clunk! Mrs. Teeth releases me and staggers to the side. Aimless has bopped her on her ugly head with his beautiful guitar! He strikes her again, and I hear the sound of wood preparing to crack. She screams with rage, and fixes Aimless's tiny frame in her murderous eyes, grinding her disgusting teeth.

And then the other thing: an explosion in Heaven.

FLAMING FAT PEOPLE FALL FROM THE SKY

There's a bright white flash, and for a moment my vision is full of blinking pink pain and squirming lines. I rub the heels of my hands against my face as pink lightning slowly subsides to sky-orange throbbing. Eventually I can see points in the orange plane: high up over the shit-dark sea, there are tumbling, burning obese bodies, growing larger, falling down out of the sky, trailing black smoke.

Mrs. Teeth sees them too, and the sight throws her into religious ecstasy. She hurls herself to the ground and moans, screaming "Forgive them! Masters, forgive them!" She tears at her hair, bashes her face against the scrap-strewn ground, and starts to weep.

The fat people loom larger in the sky now. At least a dozen of them are falling down on us.

Aimless shouts "Submarine!" and scurries over the edge of the cliff, climbing down to his battered Caravan with the battered guitar over his shoulder. Given the choice of following Aimless or remaining with Mrs. Teeth, I decide in a heartbeat. But once in the van, I can see we are well and truly trapped.

Aimless rolls up the windows, adjusts some dead knobs on the dashboard, buckles himself into the driver's seat, and looks out over the sea. The fat people are about to splash down. The first one strikes far out to sea, and with a massive crash it explodes, tossing blubber into the sky.

Aimless asks me if I want to smoke some drugs. Never have I wanted this more.

Through the smoky haze of the Caravan's atmosphere, I see a tidal wave of crap rising up on the horizon, and other flaming fat people shooting over to land behind us, striking the land in booming impacts. The scrap metal cliffside rattles and shifts. Either we will be dropped into the sea and drowned, or flattened by a tidal wave, or else the trash will fall on us and suffocate us.

I'm grinning with relief as I buckle my seat-belt. All of these deaths are so much nicer than being eaten by Mrs. Teeth.

Aimless is grinning with excitement. He's going to meet his girlfriend in the shit-dark sea.

The wave strikes the cliff, and we're flipped over as we plunge down, down, down into the ocean of excrement. The roar of explosions, crashing metal, distant screams, and the loud moaning of Mrs. Teeth are all suffocated in a cold wet plop. All is stinking blackness, while we wait to hit the bottom. Aimless peers through the glass into the sea of crap, looking for fish.

Time passes. Feces seep in slowly through cracks in the floor. The vehicle bobs and sways. We smoke more drugs. There's nothing else to do.

I tell Aimless that I'm really enjoying dying like this. This is almost beautiful.

Aimless asks me if I still think his girlfriend is fat.

I wonder when the ocean is going to crush us.

After a while, I hear the slapping of waves against the roof of the van. We are floating. But we can't see through the windows because they're slathered with feces. And the bottom of the van is filling up, slowly but surely, with the ocean's diarrhea. Aimless unbuckles himself, opens the hatch in the roof and climbs out. I follow.

Our submarine is floating on the ocean, far from home. Shit surrounds us on all sides, and the smell is twice as revolting as it is on land. But the sun is shining in the orange sky, and not far away we see a shape on the surface of the water.

It is the bobbing, charred body of a fallen fat person, still smoldering. A woman, perhaps.

Very slowly it bobs closer, face down in the slime, while gently sloshing waves of shit lap higher against the side of the van. The roof of the vehicle is slick and treacherous, so we stand perfectly still, even as the van begins to tip, ever so slowly.

The massive black corpse is our only salvation. I don't know how to swim, but as I slide into the shit-black sea I thrash my weak, gangly limbs and wave my trash stick in an effort to push myself towards the fat person's body. I manage to keep my head mostly above the waves, and soon I am climbing the hot fragments of the fat person's burned-up pearl necklace, clambering up onto its deflated back. I collapse, heaving and choking, but safe. But where is Aimless?

Aimless is still standing atop his capsizing submarine, gazing out over the waves, ignoring the fact that he's about to drown, strumming his guitar. Oblivious to danger, that's Aimless.

"GERTIE!" he sings over the waves. "GERTIE BABY SWEETIE!"

If any imaginary whales can hear him shouting, they're keeping mum about it.

After much screaming, I finally convince him to throw me a line: a knotted-together collection of short lengths of twenty kinds of rope. His rope collection.

Using it, I haul his van alongside the bloated body, and he hops aboard, guitar in one hand, telescope in the other, just as the vehicle rolls upside-down and bubbles under. Aimless stares down in dismay as the sucking whirlpool steals his submarine, home to his nautical-supplies collection, his collection of vintage soda cans, his dead insect collection, his rubber snake collection, his charts, his dreams and his drugs. All his riches, his life's work, slithering down into the shit-dark sea.

"Don't worry," I tell him. "Gertie's going to love it."

With my trash stick I scrape a hole in the back of the fat person, through its expensive dress, its expensive blouse, its expensive blubbery skin. Beneath that is an expensive metal shell which blunts my stick. My father told me the fat people were floating castles full of food and money. But even in death they won't share it with us.

I'm hungry. The fat person's skin itself is delicious, especially the parts that have been char-broiled in the sky. The flame-roasted Prada dress is tougher than most clothing I've eaten, but not bad.

We sit on the floating fat woman's back—our own private island, warm, soft, round, upholstered in wool and food. We watch the urine sun sink down into the toilet Earth. Our bellies are full, and we're free.

That night the sky is clear and I can see the sky full of perfect stars. The stars are the only things I know that don't have shit all over them. They're beautiful. I would give anything to prevent the fat people from soiling them, but I'm not hopeful.

Aimless sings to his girlfriend for a while, and then we both lie down to sleep.

MARTHA HILTON-TRUMP THE TWELFTH

In the middle of the night, a booming, blubbery, gurgling panic of a voice starts screaming beneath us:

"Lice ... maggots! Get them off me!"

It appears that the floating fat person is not quite dead.

"Parasites! Daddy!"

For a moment I see my latest death: drowning in shit, while the fat person pisses on me. But it remains motionless.

"Daddy! I'm stuck! Help me right now! They're eating me!"

Not a twitch from the giant fat fingers. Not a nod from the huge floating head. I stab into the ground with my trash stick.

"Ow! Stop it!"

Stab, stab, stab.

"OW! Daddy! Mommy!"

And still, it doesn't move.

Stab! Stab, stab, stab! A giant fat bastard is crying now! The ones who ate so many of us, the ones who ate my father, who shat on my family! Stab, stab! It cries out in pain and yet it's still powerless! The ones who humped each other screaming in the sky for hours, while we buried our heads in the shit to block out the sound ... the ones who fucked up the world ...

Stab! Stab! Stab!

Then Aimless puts a hand on my stabbing stick. He looks pained, worried.

The anger drains out of me in an instant. We listen to the pathetic, booming sobs of fat pain and fat fear. So human.

"I'm sorry," I say.

"Yeah, right!" it sneers. "Parasite! Maggot! Let me go! My daddy is going to eat you! Waaaaaaah!"

Eventually it stops crying. It tell us its name: Martha Hilton-Trump the Twelfth. It tells us it's one of the richest women in Heaven, it's college-educated, and its father, Danforth Hilton-Trump the Eleventh, is an extremely powerful and important fat person who is going to eat us. We take turns watching the sky with Aimless's telescope, but no fat people are approaching to eat us at this time.

I tell Martha my name is Cheeseburger, and she laughs. So I stab, just a little bit. This upsets Aimless, but I hate when people laugh at my name.

Aimless asks Martha Hilton-Trump if she sees any whales down in the ocean. And Martha Hilton-Trump the Twelfth laughs some more.

Night turns back to day. The sky is still empty of fat people. Aimless and I fix breakfast, to the loud protestation of Martha Hilton-Trump.

"AAAAAAA!" she gurgles. "Daddy! They're eating me!"

"We're eating a tiny, small piece of your clothing," I say. "Shut up."

"Ow! It's mine! And you're eating it!"

"Why not? You're dead anyway."

She is silent for a while, as thick waves of shit lap against her body, as her greasy shit-soaked hair floats out around her face-down head like a blonde carpet, as we eat her dress and welcome the day.

Then the weeping begins. No more threats, no more complaints, just loud, hacking, heaving sobs that swell into loud bawling, retreat back to sobbing, swell and retreat.

We sit and listen to this all day. We scream at her to shut

up! We stamp on her flesh, pound her, stab her, pull her hair, but the wailing carries on. I wrap long strips of her shitty fried clothing around my head to block out the sound, but the sound is too loud.

Such pain! Such anguish! Such terrified misery! Never did I cry as loud or as long as this, not when the fat people ate my father, not when Mrs. Teeth ate my mother, never. Oh, how the sobs of this enormous fat woman claw at the armor of my soul!

The fat people are sadder than we are; they have so much more to lose.

Eventually, to block out the noise, Aimless starts to strum his guitar as loud as he can. Finding a tune, he sings a lullaby for Martha Hilton-Trump the Twelfth:

Sleep pretty baby,
darling, sleep,
Rock on the tide
of the warm dark deep.

Your Daddy will come,
in the morning you'll ride.
Sleep pretty darling
and rock on the tide

Sleep pretty baby,
rock on the tide
Your Mommy is waiting
at home in the sky

At home in the sky,
your Mommy will keep.
So rock on the tide,
and sleep, baby, sleep.

He sings this over and over, strumming the guitar, and Martha Hilton-Trump the Twelfth seems to hear it. The sobbing boils away slowly as night falls, receding into deep wracking coughs, and then silence. But Aimless keeps on playing his guitar for hours, as the sun goes to sleep in its bed of shit, and even the stars lower their orange screen and come out to listen.

The next morning, the dead fat person called Martha Hilton-Trump has changed her dead fat-person tune. Now she wants to know Aimless's name, and where Aimless's from, and what it was like for Aimless growing up in a stinking pile of shit instead of a fluffy floating cloud of food and money. And he tells her some stories about his youth, and she says "Oh, you poor dear!" and "I never even imagined!" And she tells us some stories from her youth, all of which are revoltingly luxurious, even the supposedly bad parts.

Martha Hilton-Trump says she likes Aimless's singing. She asks for more. And for a whole day, she doesn't once threaten us with being chewed up and swallowed by her rich daddy.

I think Martha Hilton-Trump the Twelfth is in love with Aimless.

But she has nothing to say to me.

THE BLOODY HATCHET

All this time, we have been taking turns watching the skies with the telescope, waiting for the arrival of Martha Hilton-Trump's father, or any other fat people. When we see them, we know we're dead. But so far we don't see them.

However, that afternoon, we see something else: a shape on the horizon.

A ship!

Father told me about ships. I've even seen ships. Aimless had half of a book about ships somewhere in his submarine. They are like big floating boxes with sticks coming out of them, and on the sticks are bags of wind. And this is one of them, a sailing ship, sailing to meet us. Atop the tallest spire it flies two flags: one red, one black.

Aimless gives Martha Hilton-Trump the news, and Martha starts to cringe and whinge and weep all over again.

"It's the Bloody Hatchet! The terror of the shit-dark seas! Daddy!"

It grows slowly on the horizon, at the rate toadstools used to grow before we ate all the toadstools. It takes most of an hour to reach us. Fat person Martha Hilton-Trump is inconsolable the whole time. The Bloody Hatchet is a scavenger ship, she tells us, a zombie ghost ship that picks apart the dead and rapes the living. The ship's insane crew never stops laughing. "They'll flay me and fillet me!" says Martha.

"Why doesn't your fat daddy just eat them for you?" I ask. And Martha starts bawling.

187

She begs Aimless to protect her. As if Aimless could do anything with his little guitar against a ship full of laughing zombies.

Slowly, slowly, the Bloody Hatchet looms closer. It's a beautiful ship, fast and tall. Through the telescope I can make out shapes of people on the bow, staring back at us through their own telescopes. Two of them wave. I wave back. They seem friendly.

"They'll boil my bones! They'll steam my spleen!" Martha is howling in fear now, as Aimless frantically strums on the guitar, trying to calm her down.

The ship glides toward us. The people on the deck are still waving their greeting. I can hear their laughter. I can see their faces now.

And on the very bow of the ship, arms outstretched to embrace us, I see a member of my family! My aunt!

Mrs. Teeth!

"Hallelujah!" she cries.

THE PEOPLE'S COMMITTEE FOR RAPING AND PILLAGING

The Bloody Hatchet pulls up alongside Martha Hilton-Trump; its pirates swing down from the deck on ropes, happy, laughing, eager to meet us. They are all so nice! And so well-fed! They are muscular and tan and strong, you can tell they eat well. And they wear clothing: ragged red sweaters and tattered black trousers, all of it warm and beautiful. They're so healthy, so alive. They shake our hands, pat our backs, and offer us water.

Water! I've heard of it, but never seen it. It's the cleanest thing I've ever tasted.

Mrs. Teeth smiles from the deck, waving down at me, drooling.

The largest of the pirates boards us. He is a huge tree of a man, wearing a heavy black coat and a black beret with one gold-embroidered red star. He introduces himself as People's Captain Slasher-Jones, the chairman of The People's Committee for Raping and Pillaging. He bows a long, elegant bow, and asks us how long we've been stranded, if we're sick, if we're thirsty, and if we'd like to come on board to drink grog and dance a jig in celebration of our rescue.

Mrs. Teeth is hopping up and down with mad glee, waving at me, blowing kisses. Aimless sees her too, but says nothing.

While People's Captain Slasher-Jones congratulates us on our impressive catch, and tells us how thrilled he would be to take us aboard and introduce us to the members of the Steering Subcommittee and the Jig Subcommittee and the Grog

Subcommittee, a team of men from the Pillaging Subcommittee are already stripping Martha Hilton-Trump of valuables. Using long pole-hooks, they expertly snag the pearl necklace, sever it from her neck and hoist it on deck. Then they lasso an arm, hauling it up from the fecal depths, and strip it of a ladies' Rolex, some gold rings and a few other giant baubles of gold and silver. The pirates gather around the pile of booty on the deck, whooping with joy.

Through this all, Martha Hilton-Trump remains silent, playing dead. Through it all, Mrs. Teeth leers at me from the deck, drooling with excitement.

The People's Captain is waiting for our answer. He says if we join the pirate crew, we will sail together, battling the fat people and living on the sea. He says I can be the People's Watchman, riding on the top of the mast with my telescope, and Aimless can be the People's Singer-Songwriter, composing some desperately needed new jigs, subject to the approval of the Jig Subcommittee.

Aimless asks the captain: what will happen to our fat person?

Captain Slasher-Jones is sympathetic to Aimless's concerns. He places his beret over his heart and solemnly swears that absolutely nothing will happen to Martha Hilton-Trump without a plebiscite of the People's Pillaging, Raping, Devouring and Jettisoning Subcommittees.

All around us, the pirates are yelling: join us! Please, join us!

I stand at the edge of Martha Hilton-Trump's expansive ass and gaze deep down into the shit-dark sea. I've always known I'd end up down there. The only question has been when.

I look to Aimless. Aimless stares into the hole of his guitar, thinking.

But what choice do we have?

When we announce our decision, the pirate host shouts a unanimous "Hurrah!"

Then, Martha Hilton-Trump the Twelfth commences to weep.

STATUS REPORT FROM THE PEOPLE'S LOOKOUT SUBCOMMITTEE

For three days I have sat on the top of this pole. I will probably die here.

For three days Aimless and I have been pirates. As soon as I climbed on deck, Mrs. Teeth chased me around the ship, while all the pirates laughed. So I scurried up this pole with my telescope and my poking stick. Captain Slasher-Jones says my job is to keep the lookout. I am the Special Investigator of the People's Lookout Subcommittee.

With one eye I gaze out across the shit-dark sea with the telescope, confirming the ocean's constant, stinking emptiness, and the sky's curious lack of marauding fat people. With my other eye I watch Mrs. Teeth, who leers up at me from the bottom of the pole, making kissy-faces.

Mrs. Teeth can't reach me here—she's too thick and clumsy to climb this pole. If she tries, I will poke her eyes out with my stick.

But she waits for me. Sometimes she wraps herself around the mast and humps it, and it shakes, and I must hold on with all my might.

The other pirates pay her no heed, except for Captain Slasher-Jones. Three times a day, the Captain emerges from his cabin, marches to the base of this mast, and shouts up to me: "WHAT HO, LOOKOUT OF THE PEOPLE?"

Three times a day, I shout down to him, as instructed: "NOTHING HO, PEOPLE'S CAPTAIN." And he laughs, and Mrs. Teeth laughs, and he gazes longingly into her eyes. Then he

192

struts around the deck, inspecting the work of the other pirates, shouting, laughing, acting tough and important. It's plain to see he's trying to impress her.

Yesterday I saw Mrs. Teeth vanish into the Captain's cabin for a short while, and I heard horrible screams and clatter. I was terrified; I thought she was eating him. I could have slid down and run away at that moment, if I had anywhere to run to. But she returned soon enough, giggling, dressed in rags, her hair matted on her sweaty face, and then continued her leering as if she'd never left. A few minutes later, Captain Slasher-Jones crept out of the cabin and wandered in a different direction entirely, to peals of laughter from the other pirates.

They find everything funny, these pirates. Everybody is always laughing on this ship, except for me and Aimless ... and Martha Hilton-Trump the Twelfth, if you count fat people.

Martha Hilton-Trump trails the boat by a long rope tied to her hair, but her loud, desperate moaning and burbling still reaches us. It comes and goes throughout the day, deafening at times. I can tell the crew is growing irritated with her. Her misery interferes with their laughter. The only coherent word she ever speaks is "Daddy!"

Aimless sits at the stern, watching Martha Hilton-Trump as she bobs on the reeking waves, strumming his guitar for her. His song is sad and plaintive, but a few pirates from the Jig Subcommittee gamely attempt to dance to it, trying their best to ignore the sobs of the giant floating fat person, even when the weeping drowns out Aimless's little wooden guitar.

The pirates have given us clothing, and water, and committee assignments, and for all that I am grateful, especially the water. But hospitality is only worth so much at the top of a cold pole.

And their customs are strange. When I shat from the

here, down onto the deck and all over Mrs. Teeth, there was much laughter. But later the Captain scolded me.

"We be a civilized people," he said. "And this be the People's Ship. Keep it tight!" As if every single plank of the deck, every single particle of this ship and of the earth, did not have shit all over it already.

I was not punished, except that now I must shit in a bucket on a rope, which I am then required to empty over the edge of the ship. I must hold the bucket under myself with one hand while I shit, while I hold onto the pole with the other hand, while Mrs. Teeth stares directly up into my asshole.

Thankfully, I haven't had to do this often. We've had no food for three days.

At night, after Martha Hilton-Trump sobs herself unconscious, face down in the shit-dark sea, and after Mrs. Teeth curls up around my mast and falls asleep drooling, and after the pirates have sung each other lullabies and laughed themselves to sleep ... then, Aimless tiptoes to the mast and quietly puts drugs in my shit-bucket, and I haul them up and smoke them, and we talk.

Aimless says I mustn't get the wrong idea. He's still in love with Gertie the Whale. Martha Hilton-Trump he only pities. She lost everything there is to lose, he says. She is young, he says, and foolish.

And rich, I add. And tasty.

Aimless has made special petitions to the Raping and Devouring Subcommittees, asking them to postpone their raping and devouring. He told them they can ransom her for infinite treasure when her Daddy finally comes. The pirates are intrigued by this idea, but also very hungry.

"If Martha's daddy were coming," I said, "we'd all be dead by now."

It's a perfect mystery: why did the fat people explode? Why did they fall to earth? One day they were up there, the next day they were gone. Are they dead? Or will they rise again? Aimless has asked Martha Hilton-Trump what happened, but the question only makes her cry.

Even if Mrs. Teeth eats me in my sleep, even if the pirates toss me in the sea for shitting on their deck, there is one thing on this ship that was worth coming for, and that is this excellent view of the overhanging stars. Since the fat people exploded, the sky has been clear of orange smoke at night. The winking, glittering stars overhead are my blanket. Aimless agrees: the stars are cleaner and more beautiful than anything on earth. I wish I could keep the fat people away from them.

A DREAM WITH MY MOTHER'S VOICE IN IT

It seems I am going mad, just like Aimless.

At night I tie ropes around my arms and legs so I can sleep without falling into the jaws of Mrs. Teeth. For three nights I've fallen asleep this way, a sack of bones hung to dry under the precious stars, and each night I've had the same dream. I dreamed I heard the voice of my mother, a woman I've never met.

In this dream, I am watching the sky with my telescope, when each of the stars in the sky explodes, one by one, with a huge flash and a loud bang. Then the sky itself bursts into flame. Fire and smoke and feces and burning guitars rain down on the shit-dark sea. The pirates hide under deck, but I am still dangling from the mast. The wind whips me as the ocean churns. Huge waves of shit juggle the Bloody Hatchet. Shit crashes over me, shit pounds the deck. I am whipped back and forth as the creaking ship spins and dips and shudders, tumbling under breaking waves of shit. My pole becomes slick with crap; I lose my grip and I'm tossed into the ocean. I thrash around, grasping at the smoldering guitars that float on the surface. I grab several of them and try to lash their strings together to build a raft. But then a huge wave pounces on me, shoving me down, down, down into the sickening turd. I can't see, I'm choking. The hideous reeking muck squeezes into my eyes, my ears, my nose. I open my mouth and it pours down my throat, as I sink deeper and deeper ... but then I fall through the bottom of it, and open my eyes.

Under the ocean of shit there is another, larger ocean—an ocean of transparent clean water! Water that washes the shit out of my eyes, my skin, my fingernails, my hair, my red pirate shirt

196

and my black pirate pants. I inhale, drinking in this water, and it rushes through my body, destroying all the filth in me, filling me with life. And, drinking it, I can fly!

I zoom in crazy circles, surrounded on all sides by life—a world of animals floating all around me: horses, snakes, giraffes, leopards, dinosaurs, jackalopes. All the animals we killed are still alive here, swimming in circles. And flowers, and trees, and cars, and toadstools too, all twirling through space, drifting gently in the pure, delicious water that surrounds us. A black and white cat rubs against my feet and swims away. Two goldfish chase past me, swimming upside-down. They're so beautiful I can't even eat them.

The water itself glows, bathing everything in a pure shimmering moonlight. And down below me, a brighter light beckons, shining up like an upside-down moon on the ocean floor.

I swim deeper, faster, toward the glowing thing that hangs there in the bottom of the sea. It is like a huge glowing fat person, but in the shape of a fish. Its skin seems to be made out of the full moon itself, all blue-gray and glowing, and covered with tiny craters. It wears no clothing, no jewelry, not even any arms or legs. It only has fins, a tail and a huge, smiling face with beautiful blue-green eyes.

The glowing fat fish sings to me in my mother's voice.

It tells me its name is Gertie.

NUNS HO!

On the morning of the fourth day, we sighted the Ship of Nuns.

As on the first three mornings I awoke upside-down, tangled in a dangling strangulation of ropes that cut into my limbs and left my fingers and toes numb. As on the first three mornings, the first thing I saw when I opened my eyes was Mrs. Teeth, patient as gravity, batting her eyes and licking her lips.

After righting myself and rubbing the pain out of my arms, I took up my telescope to check the condition of the emptiness. But I was startled to see something quite near on the horizon: a ship, with tattered sails!

Through the telescope I saw women on the deck of the ship, kneeling around the mast, clothed in long black dresses and long black hats, all gazing up wistfully at the place where their sails had been. And up there, lashed to the mast of that ship, was a desperate-looking naked man. With his limp arms outstretched on the rigging, he appeared at least half-dead.

When I heard the women shouting "Hallelujah!" at him, I could not help but sympathize.

Captain Slasher-Jones stormed onto the deck. "LOOKOUT OF THE PEOPLE!" he cried. "WHAT HO?"

"NUNS, CAPTAIN!" I cried. "NUNS HO!"

I pointed out the ship. Every pirate rushed to the railing to see, and to cheer, and to laugh. They hoisted the sails and caught a wind, and we made for our rendezvous with the Ship of Nuns.

MY POSITION ON THE EATING OF NUNS

I would have preferred not to eat them. In a world of choice, a world of options, I would have opted out of the nun-eating. Although they were delicious, and I was hungry.

But I would have preferred not to. When the strong, friendly pirates pulled alongside the nun-ship, waving and smiling and greeting them so politely, I expected ... I don't know. Something other than what I saw, from above.

I have never seen so many women raped in one day.

I'm so tired of this life.

My father's mother used to tell him incredible stories of the past when he was small, and when I was small my father would tell these same stories to me. Stories about the Easy Times, the Age of Stuff, when every person got to decide what to do with their own life. In the times before shit, before poverty, even the littlest people were incredibly rich and wealthy and happy and stupid. When Grandma was young, Father told me, life was an endless banquet of options, a feast of fascinating choices with exotic names: Right, Wrong, Democrat, Republican, War, Peace, Regular, Unleaded.

All day long, every single day of her life, the waiters of the world brought steaming trays of fine, delicious, enticing lifestyle options to my grandmother's table, each fresh and ripe with unfolding possibility. All my grandmother had to do was pick the ones she wanted. That was her life! Can you even imagine it?

As the People's Committee for Raping and Pillaging seethed over the helpless nuns, making meat of them, stripping them of clothing and then of flesh, drowning their screams with mad laughter and darkening the decks with their blood, I found, finally, that I could no longer watch.

And when I looked away, I caught the eye of the other man, the man on the mast of the other ship. He was still just barely alive, though the whole height of his mast was painted red with his blood. Blood seeped in rivulets from wounds in his hands and feet. Looking closer, I saw the nails in his flesh.

I asked the man how he ended up in such a fix, but he never told me. He only begged for mercy.

"Please, sir," he croaked in a weak, bloody whisper, "please spare my sisters. Eat me instead! I'm delicious and tasty, I promise! I'll give you my body gladly, but please have mercy on the women. They are innocent and good! I'm crispy and tender and full of magic! I'll feed you all, with just my body. Please, let them go! You'll live forever if you eat me instead!"

I told him he was asking the wrong guy.

A moment later, the People's Captain cut him down and fed him to Mrs. Teeth.

Here's the thing: I am completely different from everybody else in the world, in a way that completely does not matter. In Grandma's time, in a world of choice, a world of either-or, I could be the People's Captain. I know it. I could live, grow and flourish in a world like that. I could hew to a righteous path. Or I could even hew to a terrible, hideous path, in a world where I get my choice of paths for hewing. If I could have chosen nun-eating, then I would have gone forth and boldly eaten nuns until I died. I have a strong mind. My ancestors' decision-making power still flows in my blood. I could do everything I chose to do, if I could choose.

But all the choices worth choosing drowned in the shit-dark sea a long, long time ago.

Live or Die?

Kill or Be Killed?
Starve or Eat Nuns?
These are the only items on my menu.

Aimless ate no nuns. He refused their meat, though I know he's more hungry than I am. Even at sunset, when the members of the Jig Subcommittee slow-roasted a nun-foot on a spit, just for Aimless, and offered it to him on a jeweled plate, he refused and turned away. I watched him clamber over the stern, lowering himself carefully onto the head of Martha Hilton-Trump. The jilted pirates ate the foot without him, and did not try to follow.

Martha Hilton-Trump saw nothing of what happened to the Nun Ship—her eyes are still pressed against the shit-dark sea —but did she overhear? I wonder what Aimless will tell her.

He's stopped strumming his guitar. In the moonlight I can see him crouched cross-legged on Martha Hilton-Trump's floating head, whispering something to her, I don't know what.

Tonight I hate the stars. Tonight the stars are ugly stupid specks, flaws in the darkness. They can't help me and they never could. Tonight I'm hanging upside-down in my bed of ropes, watching Mrs. Teeth suck the marrow from another man's bones while the giant floating fat woman wails and the mad pirates laugh and the never-ending world of filthy shit reeks in all directions. Tonight I stare out over the shit-dark sea watching the nun-ship burn. I eat my piece of nun, and wait for Gertie the Whale to take me down.

MORNING OF THE SHITTIEST DAY

This morning it rained shit, laptop computers, Leatherman Super-Tools, and blood. A laptop struck me in the hand, I think it broke a bone in my wrist. One Leatherman Super-Tool smashed a porthole in the People's Captain's Cabin. Captain Slasher-Jones came storming out, demanding a report.

"SHIT HO, PEOPLE'S CAPTAIN!" I cried. "SHIT AND LAPTOPS!" All the men took cover, while I hung in the mast, weathering the storm. For better or worse, I'm still alive.

The fat people are back. I can see them through my telescope high, high up in the orange sky, zooming angrily to and fro, swarming the way startled wasps once swarmed, before we ate all the wasps. The fat people are back, and they're angry.

I shouted the news to the whole crew this morning, including Aimless, but Aimless is busy. From my vantage point I can see that he has opened some kind of hatch in the back of Martha Hilton-Trump's giant skull, and climbed inside her head. What he's doing in there I don't know, but he'd better not let Daddy catch him.

Nobody missed the fat people, but they have returned anyway.

After the squall, Mrs. Teeth found a Leatherman Super-Tool on deck, licked it clean of shit and blood, and now, whenever the Captain isn't watching, she uses its tiny saw-blade to saw away at my mast. The tiny, persistent scratching sound reverberates up through the pole and scrapes at my ears. Scrape, scrape, scrape. Saw, saw, saw. It will take her a long while to saw through all that

202

wood, but Mrs. Teeth is persistent.

While she saws daintily away at my mast, she bats her pinched-together eyes at me, and asks when I'm going to come down and marry her. And then fuck her.

Honesty is my handicap. I tell her: never in a hundred years will I do either of those things.

Saw, saw, saw. Scrape, scrape, scrape.

My broken wrist has swelled up like a tiny fat person. I can't use my right hand. With my left hand I am tightening the ropes around myself, lashing myself to the mast as tightly as I can.

The pirates aren't laughing anymore. They're sharpening their pole-hooks and their harpoons, preparing for battle. The People's Captain barks orders from the bow, while the men hoist heavy iron cannons up onto the main deck. The shit-stained sails are spread tight under heavy wind. The mast groans and flexes as we rush across the slick water.

Scrape, scrape, scrape.

THE MOTION OF THE PEOPLE'S CAPTAIN

The wind is howling now. The snapping of the sails hurts my ears. Boiling black clouds are filling up the orange sky, and the shit-dark sea is lumpy and churning.

The People's Captain stalks the deck with a sword and a bottle of vodka, delivering an inspirational message to the People's Committee for Raping and Pillaging.

"Comrades," he says, "look at the sky! See how it quivers and sags! See how Heaven itself quakes at our approach!

"Comrades, the sea! How it trembles! How it roars! See how the Bloody Hatchet strikes fear into the waves themselves!

"Comrades, look around you, at our terror ship, at the cruel blades and the heavy cannon and the long, nasty harpoons. Look at the nun-meat piled high on the stern, at the blood boiling in pots by the cannon, at the stacks of nun-heads ready to be dipped in the boiling blood, loaded in the cannons and fired! Do we not strike a fearsome figure? Are we not pirates to the bone?

"Comrades! Today is the day I've promised you! Today we take the fight to the fat skies! Today we will storm the pearly gates! Today we will shit in the eyes of God, and feast upon the flesh of the infinite! We will plunder the vaults of Heaven! We will pillage the Garden of Eden! We will fart in the face of power, and piss in the mouth of destiny!

"Some may die. Nay, many may die. Nay, nay, all shall die, I promise it. Nay, even that is false. Know this, Scalawags of the People: we are all dead already! Every one of us is dead, for ours is a ghost ship, a ship that fishes drowned souls up out of the shit-dark sea, and grants them one last chance for glory!

"Today, the Bloody Hatchet sails home to oblivion! Oblivion and glory!"

"Comrades! I make a motion that we strike, that we fight, that we die! In the name of the People! For the glory of the People! For justice! For freedom! And for the love of bloody vengeance! Who among ye might second this motion?"

A hearty cheer rang out from the crew.

"Who among ye might place this motion on the agenda?"

Another cheer rang out.

"Who among ye might move this motion to the top of the agenda, given its priority?"

Another cheer.

"Who among ye might discuss this motion?"

Then began much shouting and confusion, as the People's Committee carried the Captain's motion through their arcane decision-making process. The motion was affirmed, recorded, amended, reaffirmed and re-recorded. Debate was extended, although there was no opposition. Fiscal impact and environmental impact were both assessed. Fingers were wiggled. It was very boring. And through it all, Mrs. Teeth scraped away at my pole from below. Scrape, scrape, scrape.

Then I noticed Aimless. He was standing waist-deep in the hatch in Martha Hilton-Trump's floating charred head, waving at me.

And I saw that the fat, toasted carcass of Martha Hilton-Trump rode very high in the water, much higher than before. And I thought I heard a rumbling, a mechanical hum, in the tone of her voice.

What is Aimless doing in there?

The ire of the fat people is rising. The clouds are blistering brown-black smoke dragons, pregnant with thunderbolts. Hot

205

diarrhea starts to drizzle down on us. The pirates have finished their plebiscite, two hours after they begun, with much laughter and much shouting.

It is finally resolved: the pirates will fight the fat sky-bastards to the death.

Mrs. Teeth is making good progress, I think. As the rough sea tosses our boat, my pole flexes farther than ever, and I sometimes hear tiny splintering crackles in the wood.

Scrape, scrape, scrape.

Martha Hilton-Trump is making ominous noises: whirring, sucking, pinging, gurgling, ticking. Aimless is in there somewhere, busying himself with something insane. Occasionally he scurries out of Martha's head, runs down her back, peers at something in the water below her huge charred buttocks, then scurries back inside. But not before waving at me.

THE FINAL SHITSTORM

Now it begins. Shit-encrusted lambskin steering wheel covers flutter down from the sky and plop on the deck. Then come shit-covered iPhones. The men slash at the sky with their swords, deflecting the hail, laughing. They've seen worse.

Then, the My Little Ponies come tumbling down, covered in feces. They bounce and skitter across the deckboards. One smacks directly on my skull, kicking me with its little plastic hooves. I feel what might be a tiny trickle of blood behind my ear, or perhaps just diarrhea

Boardgames covered in shit. Air Jordans covered in shit. It keeps coming, but the men just laugh. Really it's not so bad. We've all seen worse.

I wonder, have the fat people grown weak? Have they not yet recovered all their power?

But then come the children's bicycles. Crashing down hard and shitty, exploding into whirling pink plastic and steel skeletons when they strike. One pirate is crushed by a direct hit. Another man's throat is impaled on a seat-post decorated with plastic horses. Shrapnel flies everywhere. The captain is felled by a ricocheting Spider-Man chain guard to the face, but he regains his footing. "Fight, scalawags!" he cries as blood streams from his eye, but the smarter pirates dive below deck and cower, while the pink and black metal hail smashes apart the railings and chops at the deck. Only myself, the Captain, and Mrs. Teeth remain topside. Oblivious to the danger, Mrs. Teeth is still sawing frantically with her little metal knife. I see the blood-blisters in her hand, and the madness in her eyes.

Then a sideways-gliding pink mini-bike shoots down from on high, coming straight at me, its handlebar streamers screaming! It strikes the mast hard, just below my foot. With a rough crunch of yielding wood, the mast tips sideways a dozen degrees, settling into a wounded stoop.

The People's Captain stands on the bow, surveying the carnage with his remaining eye, as death bombs down from the sky on little girls' pink bicycles. He sees the mast teetering, and then he spots, for the first time, what Mrs. Teeth is doing and has been doing all this time with her rotten little knife.

In a glance, he sees why she has spurned him. He understands the object of her obsession, and why she is so often by the mast and so rarely at his side. He sees what love has wrought.

With a great leap Captain Slasher-Jones crosses the deck and draws his scabbard. With a wrenching scream of misery, he decapitates the woman he loves. Mrs. Teeth's hideous head tumbles through the broken railing and plops into the shit-dark sea, her animal eyes leering at me all the while.

But her headless body clings to the crooked mast, and keeps on scraping away with its little metal saw.

Scrape, scrape, scrape.

Then the storm pauses. Up in the sky, directly above us, a bright orange light boils away a hole in the clouds, as a roaring, swirling wind yanks at the broken sails. The hole in the clouds opens wider, and through the telescope I see clearly the immense Prada shoes on the fat feet of, the vast Dolce & Gabbana sport-coat around the lunar girth of, the enormous Tommy Hilfiger necktie around the angry, flabby neck of, the titanic Gucci sunglasses on the scowling evil face of ... the biggest, fattest, ugliest, meanest fat person I have ever seen in the whole of my filthy useless life. My life that is about to end.

I look to Martha Hilton-Trump, whose daddy is finally coming.

But now, with Aimless waving from the hatch in her head, Martha Hilton-Trump's body is slowly rising, fattening, re-inflating with gas, and now I see that mad Aimless has actually repaired something in her, because she rises above the waves, dripping with shit, and slowly hovers closer.

The Captain stares in shock at the oncoming family drama. Martha Hilton-Trump's charred body floats up beside me, and from the top of her head Aimless tosses to me the frayed end of his rope collection. I tug weakly on the line with my one good hand.

"Aimless!" I yell through the roaring wind. "What are you doing? You're going to get killed!"

"We're going traveling!" he yells. "Come with us! There's lots of room!"

"What about Gertie?" I ask. "Aren't you in love with a whale?"

For a little while, there's nothing but the whirling of the wind and the roar of fat engines.

"Gertie's a wonderful lady," he says. "But me and Martha have a really special thing going. I mean ... there's a kitchen in here!"

The mast teeters and creaks. Down below the Captain stares up in shock and horror, as the headless lady scrapes, scrapes, scrapes.

Love! You can't burn it, you can't eat it, you can't depend on it, or argue with it, or explain it. You can't even kill it! It just grabs you by the neck and and marches you into the shit-dark sea.

I wouldn't take ten buckets of Love for one handful of my own shit.

"We gotta make time," shouts Aimless. "Just tie the rope

around you and I'll haul you up. There's a sofa in here. And a mini-bar!"

"Go eat your fucking mini-bar!" I say. "*I'm* in love with Gertie! And *I'm* going to meet her!"

Admitting that miserable truth, I let go of Aimless's rope-collection. It twirls down to the deck below.

The horrible fat father looms over us like a toxic cloud, staring down, clenching and unclenching its fat fingers, its sunglassed face grimacing in horror. Its fat anguished voice thunderclaps in my ears:

MARTHA!

Aimless shrugs. Then he ducks back inside the head of his new girlfriend, and they rocket past Daddy into the sky.

But Captain Slasher-Jones will not be denied. He seizes the other end of Aimless's rope collection and expertly lashes it around the stout brass anchor cleat on the bow. When the slack runs out, the ship jerks violently and my broken mast tips sideways, dangling me over the edge of the ship.

Gazing down into the shit-dark sea, I search for my beloved.

With a mighty roar of Martha Hilton-Trump's engines, the Bloody Hatchet is dragged, creaking and swaying, up out of the ocean and into the sky! The pirates peer out from below deck in confusion, while the People's Captain laughs and laughs. The knots of Aimless's threadbare rope shudder as the they tighten, the fibers crackle and twist under the strain. The wind screams.

Now we rise up past the face of the fat father, its huge head twice as large as the ship. It removes its sunglasses. Where its eyes should be are two bloody, grinding metal mouths. Its third mouth gapes open, screaming with the horror of a father's love:

MARTHA!

Its seizes the ship in a stubby squeezing hand. Captain Slasher lassoes the huge fat fingers clawing at his deck. The loud ticking of three gigantic Rolex watches echoes from its wrist.

"Now, my comrades! Now!" screams the People's Captain, and the mad pirates of the Committee for Raping and Pillaging pour out from below deck and swarm over the monstrous hand, stabbing and slashing at it. They climb up its fat wrist, into the fat sleeve of its fat sport-coat, slashing and stabbing and setting fire to the fabric. Captain Slasher winds more thick ropes around the fat father's fingers and lashes them to the cleat. Two other pirates drive red-hot harpoons under its fingernails.

The powerful machinery of Martha Hilton-Trump's ascension roars still louder, straining still harder, and we rise still higher into the sky. The ratty, knotted tow-rope twitches and shudders. The fat father writhes and screams, helpless. It's so fat and round that its left arm can't reach its right to rescue it. The laughing horde of pirates surges forward up its arm, toward its fat neck and head. It flails blindly, swatting our boat against its great belly again and again, trying to flatten the crawling attackers. The hull fractures, the deckboards snap, the bow bends in upon itself, and my mast snaps cleanly free from the hull and tumbles to the broken deck, snagged in various ropes and turnbuckles. Through it all, Captain Slasher-Jones clings to the brass cleat, laughing and laughing as we rise higher and higher.

I look out over the wide horizon, shit-dark and pestilent in all directions, without a scrap of land, a scrap of anything clean or safe to cling to anywhere

Martha Hilton-Trump and her father tug against each other with all their power. From far on high, Aimless shouts my name.

CHEESEBURGER! CUT THE LINE!

Me? But I'm still strapped to this pole, unable to move, my broken hand throbbing as the mast spins around the deck, as the Bloody Hatchet whips through the sky, as the fat father howls in pain and panic, as the pirates crawl all over the fat father's face and through its hair, laughing, stabbing.

And now, the headless body of Mrs. Teeth is staggering blindly toward me, humping its way along the length of the mast, stabbing the air with its sharp little saw. Even headless she won't leave me alone!

Love!

I call to the Captain: "Cut the line!"

The one-eyed Captain sneers at me with wounded laughter. "Drown in shit, ye treacherous pond-scum!"

"Please, Captain! Cut the line! We're rising too high!"

The Captain shows me the middle finger on his free hand. "Rise high on this, ye filthy pigeon! Ye deck-crapping troglodyte!"

I recognize the sadness in his mad laughter. "What have ye got?" he cries, staring at me dumbfounded. "What speck of manhood? What did she find in ye so desirable, ye drifting dingleberry? I'm the People's Captain! And I loved her so!"

Then he releases the giant brass cleat, draws his bloody sword, and climbs toward me across the heaving deck with murder in his one good eye.

Love!

I AM ABOUT TO DIE

It seems certain that I am about to die in one of the following awful ways:

I may be raped and sawn apart by a headless madwoman.

I may be crushed to diarrhea between the rolling mast and the flying ship, or impaled on broken, twisted planks.

The People's Captain may slice me in two, in his jealousy.

The fat father may eat me, as my father was eaten before me.

I may asphyxiate in space, if we rise much higher.

I may fall down into the shit-dark sea and drown.

Or, most likely: all of these, in quick succession.

I've always expected to die, and I never held any hope that my death would be pleasant. Lately I have even longed to die, fantasized of escaping this cruel, tiring, pointless life.

But I would like to have a choice, just one choice, before I die. I would like to do one thing for any reason at all besides this awful habit of prolonging my life and this piercing hunger in my guts.

Nobody gets what they want, or what they deserve. Nobody gets anything anymore, except the fat people. For the rest of us this world is a hell of shit and pain; only the mad are suited to it.

But I demand to make a choice! I demand that one thing about this world be changed by my brief suffering. I can't die until I've left my mark! I don't care if it's selfish, but I just want to change the world in some tiny, lasting way. Any change at all would be an improvement.

The fat father writhes, and the ship heaves, and the mast skitters and rolls, and suddenly the Captain and Mrs. Teeth's body and the mast and I are piled up on the bow, on top of the big brass cleat. My arms are caught—the pain in my hand is agony! But from where I lie I can just about stretch out and lay the back of my neck across the rock-hard knot that holds Martha Hilton-Trump's tow line.

Captain Slasher-Jones is first to recover his balance and his blade.

"Kill me, Captain!" I scream! "Cut my miserable throat!"

Mrs. Teeth stumbles to her feet, gore oozing from the stump of her neck, waving her dirty saw.

"Take me, Mrs. Teeth!" I yell! "Saw off my head! And fuck me!"

I arch my head back, pressing my neck harder against the bitter end of Aimless's rope-collection. If just one of them will slice my head off, they might cut the knot as well, and set Aimless and his stupid girlfriend free.

But then, the headless body of Mrs. Teeth, instead of raping me, finds the Captain with its blind fingers. It molests him savagely, grasping at his genitals and slashing at his face.

And then Captain Slasher-Jones, instead of slicing my head off, cuts the line.

A whip-snap whistles away into the sky, and we are falling.

The fat father roars in pain. Pirates are cutting his face, cracking open his skull, crawling down his throat, and we are falling.

The Captain and Mrs. Teeth copulate on the deck of the

ship while they slice one another apart, and we are falling.

The ship shatters, the mast cracks apart and I tumble away into space, falling.

The burnt-black body of Martha Hilton-Trump the Twelfth rockets away into the starry sky.

And I am falling, falling, falling, down into the shit-dark sea to drown.

I'm so happy! I'm so ready to die!

Gertie! Baby! Sweetie! I'm coming!

GREETINGS FROM THE BOTTOM OF THE SEA!

Gertie the Whale changed my life! I really mean that. I used to be bitter and depressed, but now I've found my reason to keep living! I know it sounds corny, but you know everything they say about true love? Well, it's true.

We live together at the bottom of the sea, down here in this wonderful bubble of life. Sure, it's kind of dark and damp, but we think it's the best place in the world. It's so beautiful and alive; it's full of great scenery and really excellent food. The water is delicious, clean and healthy, and it turns out that the fungus in my belly is able to breathe it. Imagine my surprise!

Now I'm in better shape than I've ever been. I've put on weight, my skin has cleared up, and I've gotten to be a pretty good swimmer. I hardly even cough anymore. All thanks to Gertie.

I know what you're thinking: sure, she's kind of fat. But she's special!

Sometimes we float for hours, singing and gazing into each other's eyes.

Every now and then, Aimless and Martha come down to visit us. But rarely; it's tricky sneaking past their in-laws. It's always great to see them though, even if Martha is kind of annoying sometimes.

The two of them used to travel around the solar system a lot, but now they've more or less settled down on a nice crater on the far side of the moon.

Aimless keeps busy. He's been fixing up Martha; he's organized and displayed his space-junk collection in her abdomen, and remodeled the kitchen and the wet-bar. He still plays a wicked guitar, too, and he's learning the drums.

Martha plays the Sousaphone, but she's not very good.

Aimless and Gertie never talk about that romance they used to have. But they're still very fond of one another. It's funny how things work out.

Life is good, great, grand; Gertie and I are really happy ... except, if the truth be told, I really do miss my dear friend Aimless sometimes. I wish he could visit more often. I've tried to talk the two of them into moving down here, but Martha says she'd find it depressing, and I'm sure she's right.

It seems like forever ago, when Aimless and I used to dig for nautical supplies together in the mountains of trash on the crazy shitting planet's surface. I often ponder moving back up there with Gertie; she could meet my family, and maybe we could build an aquarium. But now's not the right time. The world, sad to say, is still fatally fucked and shat upon by mighty floating assholes. Except down here.

But sooner or later those fat people will choke on their own shit. We will wait them out.

That's my philosophy: things are so shitty, they can only get better!

ABOUT THE AUTHOR

Mykle Hansen's inability to have a normal reaction is key to the popularity of his surreal fiction and neo-gonzo journalism. He is the author of the acclaimed short-story collection EYEHEART EVERYTHING, the satirical novel HELP! A BEAR IS EATING ME!, several dozen 'zines, a religious self-help column in the Portland Mercury, and over fifty thousand lines of Perl.

A jack of all trades since birth, Mykle Hansen still tries to spend most of his time writing. He lives in Portland, Oregon with his wife and child, in an orange castle surrounded by a moat of man-eating chickens.

Bizarro books

CATALOG FALL 2008

Bizarro Books publishes under the following imprints:

www.rawdogscreamingpress.com

www.eraserheadpress.com

www.afterbirthbooks.com

www.swallowdownpress.com

For all your Bizarro needs visit:

WWW.BIZARROCENTRAL.COM

Introduce yourselves to the bizarro genre and all of its authors with the Bizarro Starter Kit series. Each volume features short novels and short stories by ten of the leading bizarro authors, designed to give you a perfect sampling of the genre for only $5 plus shipping.

BB-0X1
"The Bizarro Starter Kit"
(Orange)

Featuring D. Harlan Wilson, Carlton Mellick III, Jeremy Robert Johnson, Kevin L Donihe, Gina Ranalli, Andre Duza, Vincent W. Sakowski, Steve Beard, John Edward Lawson, and Bruce Taylor.

236 pages $5

BB-0X2
"The Bizarro Starter Kit"
(Blue)

Featuring Ray Fracalossy, Jeremy C. Shipp, Jordan Krall, Mykle Hansen, Andersen Prunty, Eckhard Gerdes, Bradley Sands, Steve Aylett, Christian TeBordo, and Tony Rauch.

244 pages $5

BB-001"The Kafka Effekt" D. Harlan Wilson - A collection of forty-four irreal short stories loosely written in the vein of Franz Kafka, with more than a pinch of William S. Burroughs sprinkled on top. **211 pages $14**

BB-002 "Satan Burger" Carlton Mellick III - The cult novel that put Carlton Mellick III on the map ... Six punks get jobs at a fast food restaurant owned by the devil in a city violently overpopulated by surreal alien cultures. **236 pages $14**

BB-003 "Some Things Are Better Left Unplugged" Vincent Sakwoski - Join The Man and his Nemesis, the obese tabby, for a nightmare roller coaster ride into this postmodern fantasy. **152 pages $10**

BB-004 "Shall We Gather At the Garden?" Kevin L Donihe - Donihe's Debut novel. Midgets take over the world, The Church of Lionel Richie vs. The Church of the Byrds, plant porn and more! **244 pages $14**

BB-005 "Razor Wire Pubic Hair" Carlton Mellick III - A genderless humandildo is purchased by a razor dominatrix and brought into her nightmarish world of bizarre sex and mutilation. **176 pages $11**

BB-006 "Stranger on the Loose" D. Harlan Wilson - The fiction of Wilson's 2nd collection is planted in the soil of normalcy, but what grows out of that soil is a dark, witty, otherworldly jungle... **228 pages $14**

BB-007 "The Baby Jesus Butt Plug" Carlton Mellick III - Using clones of the Baby Jesus for anal sex will be the hip sex fetish of the future. **92 pages $10**

BB-008 "Fishyfleshed" Carlton Mellick III - The world of the past is an illogical flatland lacking in dimension and color, a sick-scape of crispy squid people wandering the desert for no apparent reason. **260 pages $14**

BB-009 "Dead Bitch Army" Andre Duza - Step into a world filled with racist teenagers, cannibals, 100 warped Uncle Sams, automobiles with razor-sharp teeth, living graffiti, and a pissed-off zombie bitch out for revenge. **344 pages $16**

BB-010 "The Menstruating Mall" Carlton Mellick III - "The Breakfast Club meets Chopping Mall as directed by David Lynch." - Brian Keene **212 pages $12**

BB-011 "Angel Dust Apocalypse" Jeremy Robert Johnson - Meth-heads, man-made monsters, and murderous Neo-Nazis. "Seriously amazing short stories..." - Chuck Palahniuk, author of Fight Club **184 pages $11**

BB-012 "Ocean of Lard" Kevin L Donihe / Carlton Mellick III - A parody of those old Choose Your Own Adventure kid's books about some very odd pirates sailing on a sea made of animal fat. **176 pages $12**

   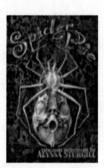

BB-013 "Last Burn in Hell" John Edward Lawson - From his lurid angst-affair with a lesbian music diva to his ascendance as unlikely pop icon the one constant for Kenrick Brimley, official state prison gigolo, is he's got no clue what he's doing. **172 pages $14**

BB-014 "Tangerinephant" Kevin Dole 2 - TV-obsessed aliens have abducted Michael Tangerinephant in this bizarro combination of science fiction, satire, and surrealism. **164 pages $11**

BB-015 "Foop!" Chris Genoa - Strange happenings are going on at Dactyl, Inc, the world's first and only time travel tourism company.

"A surreal pie in the face!" - Christopher Moore **300 pages $14**

BB-016 "Spider Pie" Alyssa Sturgill - A one-way trip down a rabbit hole inhabited by sexual deviants and friendly monsters, fairytale beginnings and hideous endings. **104 pages $11**

BB-017 "The Unauthorized Woman" Efrem Emerson - Enter the world of the inner freak, a landscape populated by the pre-dead and morticioners, by cockroaches and 300-lb robots. **104 pages $11**

BB-018 "Fugue XXIX" Forrest Aguirre - Tales from the fringe of speculative literary fiction where innovative minds dream up the future's uncharted territories while mining forgotten treasures of the past. **220 pages $16**

BB-019 "Pocket Full of Loose Razorblades" John Edward Lawson - A collection of dark bizarro stories. From a giant rectum to a foot-fungus factory to a girl with a biforked tongue. **190 pages $13**

BB-020 "Punk Land" Carlton Mellick III - In the punk version of Heaven, the anarchist utopia is threatened by corporate fascism and only Goblin, Mortician's sperm, and a blue-mohawked female assassin named Shark Girl can stop them. **284 pages $15**

BB-021 "Pseudo-City" D. Harlan Wilson - Pseudo-City exposes what waits in the bathroom stall, under the manhole cover and in the corporate boardroom, all in a way that can only be described as mind-bogglingly irreal. **220 pages $16**

BB-022 "Kafka's Uncle and Other Strange Tales" Bruce Taylor - Anslenot and his giant tarantula (tormentor? fri-end?) wander a desecrated world in this novel and collection of stories from Mr. Magic Realism Himself. **348 pages $17**

BB-023 "Sex and Death In Television Town" Carlton Mellick III - In the old west, a gang of hermaphrodite gunslingers take refuge from a demon plague in Telos: a town where its citizens have televisions instead of heads. **184 pages $12**

BB-024 "It Came From Below The Belt" Bradley Sands - What can Grover Goldstein do when his severed, sentient penis forces him to return to high school and help it win the presidential election? **204 pages $13**

BB-025 "Sick: An Anthology of Illness" John Lawson, editor - These Sick stories are horrendous and hilarious dissections of creative minds on the scalpel's edge. **296 pages $16**

BB-026 "Tempting Disaster" John Lawson, editor - A shocking and alluring anthology from the fringe that examines our culture's obsession with taboos. **260 pages $16**

BB-027 "Siren Promised" Jeremy Robert Johnson - Nominated for the Bram Stoker Award. A potent mix of bad drugs, bad dreams, brutal bad guys, and surreal/incredible art by Alan M. Clark. **190 pages $13**

BB-028 "Chemical Gardens" Gina Ranalli - Ro and punk band Green is the Enemy find Kreepkins, a surfer-dude warlock, a vengeful demon, and a Metal Priestess in their way as they try to escape an underground nightmare. **188 pages $13**

BB-029 "Jesus Freaks" Andre Duza - For God so loved the world that he gave his only two begotten sons… and a few million zombies. **400 pages $16**

BB-030 "Grape City" Kevin L. Donihe - More Donihe-style comedic bizarro about a demon named Charles who is forced to work a minimum wage job on Earth after Hell goes out of business. **108 pages $10**

BB-031 "Sea of the Patchwork Cats" Carlton Mellick III - A quiet dreamlike tale set in the ashes of the human race. For Mellick enthusiasts who also adore The Twilight Zone. **112 pages $10**

BB-032 "Extinction Journals" Jeremy Robert Johnson - An uncanny voyage across a newly nuclear America where one man must confront the problems associated with loneliness, insane dieties, radiation, love, and an ever-evolving cockroach suit with a mind of its own. **104 pages $10**

BB-033 "Meat Puppet Cabaret" Steve Beard - At last! The secret connection between Jack the Ripper and Princess Diana's death revealed! **240 pages $16 / $30**

BB-034 "The Greatest Fucking Moment in Sports" Kevin L. Donihe - In the tradition of the surreal anti-sitcom Get A Life comes a tale of triumph and agape love from the master of comedic bizarro. **108 pages $10**

BB-035 "The Troublesome Amputee" John Edward Lawson - Disturbing verse from a man who truly believes nothing is sacred and intends to prove it. **104 pages $9**

BB-036 "Deity" Vic Mudd - God (who doesn't like to be called "God") comes down to a typical, suburban, Ohio family for a little vacation—but it doesn't turn out to be as relaxing as He had hoped it would be... **168 pages $12**

BB-037 "The Haunted Vagina" Carlton Mellick III - It's difficult to love a woman whose vagina is a gateway to the world of the dead. **132 pages $10**

BB-038 "Tales from the Vinegar Wasteland" Ray Fracalossy - Witness: a man is slowly losing his face, a neighbor who periodically screams out for no apparent reason, and a house with a room that doesn't actually exist. **240 pages $14**

BB-039 "Suicide Girls in the Afterlife" Gina Ranalli - After Pogue commits suicide, she unexpectedly finds herself an unwilling "guest" at a hotel in the Afterlife, where she meets a group of bizarre characters, including a goth Satan, a hippie Jesus, and an alien-human hybrid. **100 pages $9**

BB-040 "And Your Point Is?" Steve Aylett - In this follow-up to LINT multiple authors provide critical commentary and essays about Jeff Lint's mind-bending literature. **104 pages $11**

BB-041 **"Not Quite One of the Boys" Vincent Sakowski** - While drug-dealer Maxi drinks with Dante in purgatory, God and Satan play a little tri-level chess and do a little bargaining over his business partner, Vinnie, who is still left on earth. **220 pages $14**

BB-042 **"Teeth and Tongue Landscape" Carlton Mellick III** - On a planet made out of meat, a socially-obsessive monophobic man tries to find his place amongst the strange creatures and communities that he comes across. **110 pages $10**

BB-043 **"War Slut" Carlton Mellick III** - Part "1984," part "Waiting for Godot," and part action horror video game adaptation of John Carpenter's "The Thing." **116 pages $10**

BB-044 **"All Encompassing Trip" Nicole Del Sesto** - In a world where coffee is no longer available, the only television shows are reality TV re-runs, and the animals are talking back, Nikki, Amber and a singing Coyote in a do-rag are out to restore the light **308 pages $15**

BB-045 **"Dr. Identity" D. Harlan Wilson** - Follow the Dystopian Duo on a killing spree of epic proportions through the irreal postcapitalist city of Bliptown where time ticks sideways, artificial Bug-Eyed Monsters punish citizens for consumer-capitalist lethargy, and ultraviolence is as essential as a daily multivitamin. **208 pages $15**

BB-046 **"The Million-Year Centipede" Eckhard Gerdes** - Wakelin, frontman for 'The Hinge,' wrote a poem so prophetic that to ignore it dooms a person to drown in blood. **130 pages $12**

BB-047 **"Sausagey Santa" Carlton Mellick III** - A bizarro Christmas tale featuring Santa as a piratey mutant with a body made of sausages. 124 pages $10

BB-048 **"Misadventures in a Thumbnail Universe" Vincent Sakowski** - Dive deep into the surreal and satirical realms of neo-classical Blender Fiction, filled with television shoes and flesh-filled skies. **120 pages $10**

BB-049 "Vacation" Jeremy C. Shipp - Blueblood Bernard Johnson leaved his boring life behind to go on The Vacation, a year-long corporate sponsored odyssey. But instead of seeing the world, Bernard is captured by terrorists, becomes a key figure in secret drug wars, and, worse, doesn't once miss his secure American Dream. **160 pages $14**

BB-051 "13 Thorns" Gina Ranalli - Thirteen tales of twisted, bizarro horror. **240 pages $13**

BB-050 "Discouraging at Best" John Edward Lawson - A collection where the absurdity of the mundane expands exponentially creating a tidal wave that sweeps reason away. For those who enjoy satire, bizarro, or a good old-fashioned slap to the senses. **208 pages $15**

BB-052 "Better Ways of Being Dead" Christian TeBordo - In this class, the students have to keep one palm down on the table at all times, and listen to lectures about a panda who speaks Chinese. **216 pages $14**

BB-053 "Ballad of a Slow Poisoner" Andrew Goldfarb Millford Mutterwurst sat down on a Tuesday to take his afternoon tea, and made the unpleasant discovery that his elbows were becoming flatter. **128 pages $10**

BB-054 "Wall of Kiss" Gina Ranalli - A woman... A wall... Sometimes love blooms in the strangest of places. **108 pages $9**

BB-055 "HELP! A Bear is Eating Me" Mykle Hansen - The bizarro, heartwarming, magical tale of poor planning, hubris and severe blood loss... **150 pages $11**

BB-056 "Piecemeal June" Jordan Krall - A man falls in love with a living sex doll, but with love comes danger when her creator comes after her with crab-squid assassins. **90 pages $9**

BB-057 **"Laredo" Tony Rauch** - Dreamlike, surreal stories by Tony Rauch. **180 pages $12**

BB-058 **"The Overwhelming Urge" Andersen Prunty** - A collection of bizarro tales by Andersen Prunty. **150 pages $11**

BB-059 **"Adolf in Wonderland" Carlton Mellick III** - A dreamlike adventure that takes a young descendant of Adolf Hitler's design and sends him down the rabbit hole into a world of imperfection and disorder. **180 pages $11**

BB-060 **"Super Cell Anemia" Duncan B. Barlow** - "Unrelentingly bizarre and mysterious, unsettling in all the right ways..." - Brian Evenson. **180 pages $12**

BB-061 **"Ultra Fuckers" Carlton Mellick III** - Absurdist suburban horror about a couple who enter an upper middle class gated community but can't find their way out. **108 pages $9**

BB-062 **"House of Houses" Kevin L. Donihe** - An odd man wants to marry his house. Unfortunately, all of the houses in the world collapse at the same time in the Great House Holocaust. Now he must travel to House Heaven to find his departed fiancee. **172 pages $11**

BB-063 **"Necro Sex Machine" Andre Duza** - The Dead Bicth returns in this follow-up to the bizarro zombie epic Dead Bitch Army. **400 pages $16**

BB-064 **"Squid Pulp Blues" Jordan Krall** - In these three bizarro-noir novellas, the reader is thrown into a world of murderers, drugs made from squid parts, deformed gun-toting veterans, and a mischievous apocalyptic donkey. **204 pages $12**

BB-065 **"Jack and Mr. Grin" Andersen Prunty** - "When Mr. Grin calls you can hear a smile in his voice. Not a warm and friendly smile, but the kind that seizes your spine in fear. You don't need to pay your phone bill to hear it. That smile is in every line of Prunty's prose." - Tom Bradley. **208 pages $12**

BB-066 **"Cybernetrix" Carlton Mellick III** - What would you do if your normal everyday world was slowly mutating into the video game world from Tron? **212 pages $12**

BB-067 **"Lemur" Tom Bradley** - Spencer Sproul is a would-be serial-killing bus boy who can't manage to murder, injure, or even scare anybody. However, there are other ways to do damage to far more people and do it legally... **120 pages $12**

BB-068 **"Cocoon of Terror" Jason Earls** - Decapitated corpses...a sculpture of terror...Zelian's masterpiece, his Cocoon of Terror, will trigger a supernatural disaster for everyone on Earth. **196 pages $14**

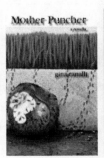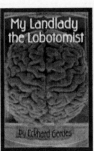

BB-069 **"Mother Puncher" Gina Ranalli** - The world has become tragically over-populated and now the government strongly opposes procreation. Ed is employed by the government as a mother-puncher. He doesn't relish his job, but he knows it has to be done and he knows he's the best one to do it. **120 pages $9**

BB-070 **"My Landlady the Lobotomist" Eckhard Gerdes** - The brains of past tenants line the shelves of my boarding house, soaking in a mysterious elixir. One more slip-up and the landlady might just add my frontal lobe to her collection. **116 pages $12**

BB-071 **"CPR for Dummies" Mickey Z.** - This hilarious freakshow at the world's end is the fragmented, sobering debut novel by acclaimed nonfiction author Mickey Z. **216 pages $14**

BB-072 **"Zerostrata" Andersen Prunty** - Hansel Nothing lives in a tree house, suffers from memory loss, has a very eccentric family, and falls in love with a woman who runs naked through the woods every night. **144 pages $11**

ORDER FORM

TITLES	QTY	PRICE	TOTAL

Please make checks and moneyorders payable to ROSE O'KEEFE / BIZARRO BOOKS in U.S. funds only. Please don't send bad checks! Allow 2-6 weeks for delivery. International orders may take longer. If you'd like to pay online via PAYPAL.COM, send payments to publisher@eraserheadpress.com.

SHIPPING: US ORDERS - $2 for the first book, $1 for each additional book. For priority shipping, add an additional $4. INT'L ORDERS - $5 for the first book, $3 for each additional book. Add an additional $5 per book for global priority shipping.

Send payment to:

BIZARRO BOOKS
 C/O Rose O'Keefe
 205 NE Bryant
 Portland, OR 97211

Address

City   State   Zip

Email   Phone

LaVergne, TN USA
18 December 2009
167417LV00002B/104/P